HONEY BAY CAFE: MAGIC SUNSETS

Second Chance Romance Mystery – Book 3

AMY RAFFERTY

© **Copyright 2022 <Amy Rafferty> — All rights reserved.**

This is a work of fiction. Names, characters, places, and incidents either are products of the author's imagination or are used fictitiously. Any similarity to actual events or locales or persons, living or dead, is entirely coincidental.

All rights reserved. No part of this publication may be reproduced, stored in, or introduced into a retrieval system, or transmitted, in any form, or by any means (electronic, mechanical, photocopying, recording, or otherwise) without the prior written permission of the copyright owner.

The author acknowledges the trademarked status and trademark owners of various products referenced in this work of fiction, which have been used without permission.

The publication / use of the trademarks is not authorized, associated with, or sponsored by the trademark owners.

Cover by Author Services by Sarah

Formatted by Author Services by Sarah

STAY UPDATED WITH ME

Thank you so much for purchasing or downloading my book! I am grateful to all my amazing readers.

To stay updated on all my latest books, newsletters, freebies and beautiful photos from the fabulous locations I write about, why not join my VIP group?

I will send you regular pictures of La Jolla Cove, San Diego and the Florida Gulf Beaches where I try to spend as much time as I can. I live in San Diego, my own 'Garden Of Eden' and I am in love with the sea and the beaches in the area. They inspire me to write lots of beachy mystery romance fiction to share with my awesome readers like you. To join me go to https://landing.mailerlite.com/webforms/landing/y6w2d2

You will be asked for your email. You also get a FREE BOOK whenever you sign-up!

FREE BOOK

To get your FREE copy of Cody Bay Inn Prequel - Nantucket Calling go to www.amazon.com/B0992NFTY1

Chapter One

THE POLICE INTERROGATION

Gemma's ribs ached, and all she wanted to do was go back to Honey Bay Manor, run a bath, and soak the pain away. It had been another crazy day on Honey Bay Island, and Gemma had had enough excitement for one day. She winced as she shifted in the uncomfortable seat at the police station.

"Why is this taking so long? And why are they keeping us here?" Gemma asked Dean. "I told the police everything I know. I'm not even sure why we are here? I'm not pressing charges."

"The police captain wants to see us," Dean told her.

"I told the officer that I don't think the driver was deliberately trying to kill me." Gemma rubbed her stiff neck. "So why does the police captain want to see me?"

"I guess we're about to find out." Dean stood

when the police captain walked over to them. "Captain James." He shook the man's hand. "This is Doctor Walker."

Gemma carefully stood up and saw the man's eyes widen with shock for a few seconds.

"I apologize for keeping you here so long," Captain James told her. "I need to review your statement again, Doctor Walker." He indicated for them to follow him down the hallway to his office.

Once they were seated at his desk, Captain James opened a folder and scanned the contents.

"Have you managed to find who the car that nearly ran Doctor Walker over belongs to?" Dean asked.

Captain James looked up from the folder and shook his head, "Unfortunately, no," he answered. "But it's a small island, and we will find it."

Gemma's eyes narrowed suspiciously, feeling that the police were lying and knew who it belonged to. As he said, it was a small island, and the car that nearly ran her down was a distinct color that, from what Gemma had seen, was not common on the island.

"You told the officer who took your statement that you didn't see the person driving the vehicle, is that correct?" Captain James said as he observed Gemma.

"Yes," Gemma confirmed.

"You also stated that you didn't see the person who pushed you out of the way." Captain James fiddled with some papers in the folder. "We asked you to wait because we were retrieving the security camera footage from the store and the parking lot," he told them, taking a photo from the folder and putting it on the desk in front of Gemma and Dean. "Are you sure you didn't see the driver?"

The photo showed Gemma standing frozen on the spot, staring at the vehicle like a deer mesmerized by headlights.

"I'm sure, but I did see my life flash before my eyes," Gemma said, annoyed that she was being questioned like she'd done something wrong.

"Doctor Walker, in this photo, you are looking right at the driver," Captain James pointed out. "You must've seen something. Was the driver a male or a female?"

"Why are you interrogating Doctor Walker about this?" Dean stopped Gemma from saying anything. "She's already told you that she didn't know the driver."

"We are merely covering all the bases, Mr. Singer," Captain James told him. "Doctor Walker was nearly killed on my island, where she is a visitor from another country."

"But she wasn't killed, and as far as I'm aware, no crime was committed," Dean pointed out. "As you stated, Doctor Walker is a guest in our country. A guest who has been more than cooperative and patient with this department." He held the police captain's attention. "So, either tell us what this is really about, or we're leaving."

"Mr. Singer, I can assure you, all we want is to make sure this doesn't happen to Doctor Walker again," Captain James told them. "We are concerned for Doctor Walker's safety. The witnesses at the scene seemed to think the driver was targeting you." He looked at Gemma.

"Why would anyone want to target me?" Gemma was getting more exasperated by the minute. "I have only been on Honey Bay Island for three days. I hardly know anyone and didn't see the driver's face."

The police captain stared at her for a few seconds before picking up another photo.

"Do you know this woman?" Captain James put a photo of a woman in front of them.

"She looks familiar," Gemma said, squinting at the heavily pixelated image. "I think she's the woman I accidentally bumped into when I went into the store looking for Dea... Mr. Singer."

Captain James put another photo on the table, this time of the incident of Gemma bumping into the woman when she went into the store.

"Are you sure you have never seen this woman before?" Captain James asked her again.

Gemma had to clench her jaw and bite her tongue as her impatience grew.

"Not until I bumped into her at the store," Gemma said. "But I think I did offend her in some way because when I said sorry, she looked at me with such —" She tried to find the word that would describe the look the woman had given her. "I don't know how to explain how she looked at me before rushing off."

"Shock or fright?" Captain James put some words forward.

"Maybe a mixture of the two," Gemma said, even though she was sure there had also been a flash of anger in the woman's eyes.

"You don't think it strange that someone you claim never to have met before would look at you in such a way?" Captain James asked Gemma.

"Not really." Gemma had gotten a lot worse, and stranger looks since arriving in Honey Bay. "I haven't gotten the warmest reception since I set foot on the island."

"Ah, yes." Captain James looked pointedly at Dean. "The case of mistaken identity at the diner."

"Does everyone on Honey Bay know about that?" Gemma looked at Dean accusingly.

"It's an island." Dean shrugged before turning his attention back to the police captain. "Why are you so interested in this woman?"

"Because we believe her to be the driver of the car that tried to run Doctor Walker down." He put another picture on the desk in front of them. "The picture is somewhat grainy in the photo, but then it is clear enough on the security camera, and the woman is looking straight at Doctor Walker."

"I still don't know who she is." Gemma sat back in the seat.

"The driver of the vehicle looks like this woman, don't you think?" He looked at Gemma and asked the questions again as if trying to trip Gemma up.

"I don't know." Gemma blew out an impatient breath. "It could be, I guess, but the driver's picture is very pixelated."

Dean agreed with Gemma about the picture not being clear enough and looked at the police captain. "Are we going to sit here for the rest of the day while you keep asking Doctor Walker the same questions?"

"After going over the security footage, I have to agree with the witnesses that say the driver deliberately targeted Doctor Walker," Captain James told them. "If she's tried to harm Doctor Walker once, there's a good chance she will try again, and we need to figure out why she wants to harm you." He sat back in his chair and addressed another question to Gemma. "Do you know of anyone who would want to harm you?"

"No," Gemma said honestly.

"One more thing before you go." Captain James looked at Gemma. "You said you didn't get a look at the face of the person that pushed you out of the way." His eyes narrowed.

"No, I didn't," Gemma said. "I told you their face was covered with a hood. I had the wind knocked out of me and was in shock, and the person was gone as quickly as they'd appeared."

Captain James looked at her for a few seconds and nodded, "Thank you for your cooperation, Doctor Walker."

Dean gave the captain a nod, grabbed Gemma's arm, picked up her almost empty water bottle from the captain's desk, and guided them to the door before they heard the captain saying,

"Oh, and Doctor Walker?"

Gemma turned to look at the man with shrewd eyes. "Welcome to Honey Bay. I hope the rest of your stay is more relaxing and less eventful."

Dean stepped back and let Gemma precede him through the door. "Don't say another word until we're in the car," he warned her.

"Why?" Gemma looked at him with a furrowed brow. "Have I done something wrong?"

"Let's go," Dean ignored her question and practically dragged her from the police station.

They were climbing into the car when Dean's phone rang. He picked it up, glanced at the number, then slid it back into the compartment between the seats. Dean put Gemma's water bottle in the cup holder next to it.

"Is something wrong?" Gemma asked him as he pulled away from the police station.

"Do you remember how I reacted when I first saw you?" Dean asked her.

"Yes, you dumped your breakfast on me," Gemma said.

"It wasn't breakfast," Dean corrected her. "I thought you were Gabby Marshall."

"Yes." Gemma nodded, and her eyes widened in realization. "Like you, the police captain was trying to figure out if I was Gabby Marshall?"

"The staff at the precinct kept asking you if you wanted some refreshments," Dean pointed out. "They were trying to find a way to figure out if you were Gabby."

"That's why you took my water bottle," Gemma guessed. "You worried they were going to run my DNA."

"Yes, that, and I would like your permission to run your DNA," Dean shocked her by saying.

"Why?" Gemma looked at him with narrowed eyes.

"A hunch," was all Dean would say before changing the subject. "I have something to show you." His eyes sparkled with mischief. "But we must wait for my grandparents to retire for the night."

"Has this got something to do with the manor?" Gemma raised her eyebrows.

"Yes." Dean grinned. "I found the keys to the locked rooms."

"No way!" Gemma exclaimed, excitement tickling her belly. She was about to ask him where he'd found them when she saw a red light blinking on his dashboard. "I think your trunk is open."

"What the..." Dean spluttered, looking at the light and then glancing in the mirror at the car's rear before pulling onto the curb. He fiddled with the seat belt. "I really have to start locking my doors."

"You don't lock your car?" Gemma gaped at him in disbelief.

"No, no one steals here," Dean said, climbing out of the car and going to the trunk.

"Really?" Gemma looked pointedly at the boot. "From where I'm sitting, unless you accidentally opened the trunk with the remote, it looks like someone wanted something from it."

Dean glared at her, pushing open the trunk. "What did you put in here?"

"The butler's table and the picture frame you made for your uncle," Gemma told him.

"Are you sure you put the picture frame in the trunk?" Gemma saw Dean fidgeting and heard the table being moved.

"Yes, I am sure. I put it in there with the table." Gemma's forehead puckered with worry lines, trying to remember if she had put the picture frame in the car. She glanced around the interior to be sure in case Dean had moved it and forgotten. Her heart twinged because she knew how important that picture frame was to Dean. "It hasn't slipped into a dark corner?"

"It's a car trunk, Gemma, not a magician's hat." Dean slammed the lid of the trunk shut, making Gemma jump. Dean slipped into the driver's seat. His jaw was set in a hard line and his hands gripped the wheel as if he wanted to shake it. "The photo frame is gone," he said through gritted teeth.

"Someone really wanted your woodwork or —" Gemma looked at Dean wide-eyed.

"Or they wanted the key because they knew what it unlocked," Dean finished the sentence. A muscle in his jaw ticked as he clenched it tighter and slammed his hand against the steering wheel.

"We only just found the key, and we had to piece together hard clues to find it," Gemma looked at him thoughtfully, chewing her lower lip. "The only way anyone else could've known is if we were being followed or..." Her eyes widened in realization for a few seconds before narrowing accusingly. "You told someone."

Dean drew in a breath, closed his eyes, and pinched the bridge of his nose before turning to look at her, "I didn't tell anyone we had found the key. I only told them I was looking for it." He ground his teeth and glared out the window.

"How would they know it was in the photo frame if you didn't tell anyone about our findings?" Gemma drummed her fingers on her leg.

"It's possible we're being followed." Dean glanced in the mirror and looked around. "But that wouldn't explain how anyone would know the key was in the photo frame."

"Unless they already knew." The thought struck Gemma. "They could've been watching the house and waiting for the perfect moment to sneak in and get it like we did."

"I doubt either of the people I told I was looking

for the files would've been surveilling my uncle's house," Dean told her.

"You told two people?" Gemma gasped in disbelief.

"Moving along..." Dean moved the conversation back to the mystery of the stolen photo frame. "It would make sense, though, if someone had known and was watching the house. They see you pick up the frame and decide to follow us."

"They wouldn't have been able to steal it at the store," Gemma pointed out. Her face fell as an image flashed through her mind. Gemma had a suspect they could add to the top of their sparse list. But she pushed the thought away as she hadn't told anyone who she'd seen. "Dean, do you think it was the woman that tried to run me down?"

"I know the photo at the police station wasn't too good," Dean looked at her. "But I don't think I've seen that woman before." His brow creased. "I don't think it was her."

Gemma looked away from Dean, closed her eyes, tilted her head, and pushed it against the headrest. She knew she was going to have to tell Dean the truth.

"Maybe we're just making a big deal over nothing, and it was simply someone wanting a picture of my uncle and his family." Dean tried to make light of everything.

"Dean, there's something I haven't told you." Gemma didn't want to open her eyes and tell him what she knew. But they had promised no more secrets when it came to their joint investigation, and this was a huge one. She looked at him, holding his gaze, and admitted, "I lied to the police."

"Why?" Dean asked, his brows creasing.

"I don't know," Gemma answered honestly. "Something inside me was cautioning me not to tell the whole truth."

"To be honest," Dean said. "I don't trust them either, especially not the new police captain."

"New police captain?" Gemma looked at him questioningly.

"Yes, his predecessor retired ten months ago," Dean shook his head. "It was a shock and surprise to everyone when he suddenly announced he was taking early retirement."

"How long had he been at the HBPD?" Gemma looked at Dean.

"I don't know exactly," Dean told her. "But I know he was quite young when he became the police captain, having taken over from his father. When I heard the news, I thought he was sick because he was only fifty-six."

"There's just something about that new police captain that I didn't like," Gemma admitted. "That is why I didn't tell him the truth about having seen the woman's face."

Dean's brows shot up in surprise as he looked at her, "You *do* know the woman who tried to run you down?"

"No, not her." Gemma shook her head. "The woman who saved me."

"It was a woman that pushed you out of the way?" Dean's jaw slackened as he stared at Gemma.

"Didn't you see her?" Gemma asked.

"No." Dean shook his head. "I came out of the store and saw you crossing the road. I hurried to catch you, and the next minute I was gripped by terror when I saw a car speeding toward you. I was trying to push through the crowd in my way, and when I got to the curb, you were plastered on the side of my car." He stared at her for a minute. "You know who she is," he realized.

"I don't know her personally." Gemma's teeth worried her bottom lip as she wondered how to tell Dean, knowing he wouldn't like what he was about to hear.

"Do I know them?" Dean pointed at his chest. "Who was it? And why are you being so weird and cagey about it?" He looked at her suspiciously. "Or rather, why wouldn't you want to tell the police about her when she saved your life?"

"Because I think it was Gabby Marshall!" Gemma blurted out.

Chapter Two

GEMMA VS. VICTOR - ROUND 2

"**G**abby?" Dean looked at her blankly before blinking and asking, "Are you sure it was Gabby?"

"Unless you know another person around town that shares the same face as mine," Gemma said sarcastically. "Then yes, I am sure."

Dean's expression went from disbelief to irritation as he turned back to the steering wheel and started the car. "What the heck is she up to?" He hissed.

Gabby watched Dean closely, and his reaction to the news about Gabby worried her. She remembered the message about a file he'd gotten on his phone.

"If Gabby knew your uncle, maybe she knew about the secret hiding place," Gemma put together a scenario for them to consider. "She could've been casing your uncle's place and trying to figure out how to get into the house." Gemma looked at the road ahead. "The security guards closed the kitchen window, and when she couldn't get in—"

Gemma and Dean looked at each, realization dawning on them, "The fire!" They chorused.

"That would mean Gabby is also looking for something your uncle had," Gemma pointed out. "She obviously saw me take the photo and followed us to the store. She couldn't take it from us there because I was in the car. Then the perfect opportunity arose at the police station." She shook her head. "I wonder what's so important to her that she'd set your uncle's house alight to get it or risk breaking into a car in front of the police station."

"I have a pretty good idea," Dean said softly and glanced at her. "I have something to tell you too."

"You've been in contact with Gabby," Gemma guessed, and Dean's stricken look confirmed it was a good guess. "The message on your phone about a file was from her, wasn't it?"

"Yes," Dean confirmed, turning into Honey Bay Manor, and driving up the long drive towards the house. "Gemma, you can't tell anyone about Gabby." He pulled the car to a stop in front of the garages and unclipped the seat belt to turn towards her. "Please, you have to promise me."

"Your family doesn't know you're in contact with her?" Gemma's eyes narrowed.

"No, and they can't know," Dean said, desperation

ringing in his voice. "I can't explain everything now, but I will tonight when we meet."

"Oh yes," Gemma said, the excitement tickling her belly again. "We get to unlock the mystery behind the locked doors of the manor."

"You make it sound like a horror movie." Dean laughed. "But yes, we will find out what the heck this place is hiding."

"Thank you for today. I can honestly say it was one of the most eventful days of my life." Gemma loosened her seat belt and opened the door but was reluctant to get out because it meant their day was coming to an end and, for some reason, Gemma didn't want it to.

"I'm sorry you passed out and nearly got run down by a car," Dean said.

"Oh, pfft," Gemma teased. "It was just another day in Honey Bay for me."

Dean laughed, "Why, Doctor Walker, one greasy meal of hamburger and fries, and look at you, making jokes. Even after everything you went through today, you look more relaxed than when you arrived."

"So, you're saying I was uptight when I arrived?" Gemma's eyes narrowed, daring him to answer her.

"Little bit." Dean indicated a small quantity with his index finger and thumb.

"Only because I was expecting friendly, fun-filled islanders but instead encountered hostile locals," Gemma pointed out.

Gemma didn't know if she was imagining things,

but he, too, seemed reluctant to leave. She felt a weird jolt in her stomach, and a tingly feeling, that made her catch her breath, filled her system. Gemma looked into his eyes, and the feeling intensified, making her throat go dry. She knew she should look away, but she couldn't. Gemma swallowed, and it tickled her throat, making her cough, which reminded her of her bruised ribs. She winced, and the spell was broken.

"Are you okay?" Dean's eyes filled with concern.

"Stupid bruised ribs," Gemma said frustratedly. "They'll heal in a few days."

"Does that mean you're not up to robbing a bank or a train with me tomorrow?" Dean joked.

"Sure, why not!" Gemma laughed. "It seems I've taken my first steps into a life of crime."

"Great," Dean said. "Then it's a date."

Dean's eyes widened like he was just as shocked as she was at the words that had slipped out of his mouth. They looked at each other, their eyes locking. Gemma felt her breath catch in her throat while her stomach felt all fluttery, and that tingly feeling made her heart race. As the silence stretched, Gemma searched for some words to break it. Then she moved slightly, and her ribs again gave a sharp throb pushing the fluttery tingling away.

"I'd better go get some ice for my ribs," Gemma said, suddenly feeling clumsy and awkward like she did when she tried to make small talk. "What time are we going to start looking through the mansion?"

She had no idea why she asked when they'd already discussed it. He was going to think she was a ditz.

"Is nine p.m. alright with you?" Dean asked, clearing his throat, and Gemma was pleased to see she wasn't the only one feeling like an awkward dolt.

"What about Sophie?" Gemma asked, stepping out of the car.

"She's with my aunt tonight," Dean said, pushing the door open. They turned to look at each other. "So, I'm all yours."

Once again, his eyes widened as if those words had slipped out before he could stop them. Gemma's stomach jolted as it had when he'd mentioned them having a date.

"I'm all yours to help you search the mansion," Dean corrected himself, and she could see him visibly squirm. He quickly glanced at his wristwatch, stepping from the car. "I'd better go get Sophie's overnight back."

"I need to ice my ribs." Gemma's hands shook as she fumbled to push herself out of the car while Dean climbed out and closed the door.

Once her jelly legs could support her, Gemma walked around to the back of the vehicle the same time Dean did, and they bumped into each other. Gemma winched in pain and nearly stumbled backward, but he caught her, drawing her to him. Gemma's emotions went into overdrive as her hands pressed up against his warm chest. Her throat went dry, and her heart hammered against her ribs when she looked up, and their eyes locked once again.

Gemma's chest rose and fell as she felt drawn to him. Tingles of excitement sparked through her, and she watched, mesmerized, as his lips drew nearer to hers. The outside world got smaller, and she tilted her chin, holding her breath in anticipation of his lips touching hers. Gemma and Dean were jolted back to reality when something solid bumped into their legs. Gemma fell sideways and hit Dean's car for the second time that day, groaning in pain when her ribs connected with the cold metal. She looked down as Rhino barked happily up at them and pranced around, his tail wagging furiously as he expressed his joy at seeing them.

"Ow!" Gemma growled when Rhino, impatient to get a pat, jumped up on her and knocked her back against the car.

"Gemma!" Dean reached for her arms to steady her; his eyes filled with concern. "Come on, let's get you safely inside."

Before she realized what he was doing, Dean scooped her up in his arms, and Gemma had no choice but to lock her arms around his neck. He carried her into the house and up the grand sweeping staircase taking two stairs at a time with Rhino right behind him, barking as if instructing Dean where to take her. Gemma felt like she'd been swept away and rescued by the handsome hero in a historical novel.

Good grief! Gemma stopped her fanciful thoughts. *Dean's right, Gemma Walker, you've become soft and mushy.*

After confirming their arrangement to meet at nine, Dean left. He hadn't been gone for long when Dora appeared at her door. She had a tray with ice for Gemma's ribs, chamomile tea, and something for her headache.

"My word," Dora huffed, walking into the room with a tray she placed beside the bed. "Dean told me what happened." She handed Gemma an ice pack. "Would you mind me taking a look at your ribs?"

"It's okay, Dora," Gemma said with a smile. "I'm sure they're just bruised."

"I'll be the judge of that," Dora said in a no-nonsense voice. "I was once a nurse practitioner, just like that young Barney." Her face relaxed when she smiled at the shocked expression on Gemma's face. "Who do you think trained the young man?"

"I did not know that!" Gemma was stunned.

"You've heard of Ms. Marshall's husband, Doc? I used to run his clinic," Dora said proudly. She helped Gemma off the bed and lifted her shirt. Her soft, warm hands gently felt around Gemma's rib cage, and she made Gemma take a few deep breaths. "There is quite a nasty bruise on your right side that we need to keep an eye on."

Dora helped Gemma fix her shirt.

"Thanks. I'll have a look when I go to bathe." Gemma sat down on the edge of the bed and picked up the tea. "Thank you for this."

"Keep icing your ribs," Dora told her. "I'll put a bath on for you and check that darn cat isn't lurking in your bathroom."

"Thank you, Dora," Gemma smiled gratefully.

Dora fussed around Gemma a little more before going to run her a bath. She appeared a few minutes later to tell Gemma her bath was ready, and as soon as Gemma was finished bathing, she'd bring Gemma's dinner to her room. Gemma finished her tea and walked into the bathroom after she left.

The smell of honeysuckle from the pile of frothy bubbles in the long claw-footed tub tickled her senses. Gemma sighed in delight at the sight, looking forward to climbing into the scented froth and soaking her aching ribs. She was about to undress when something streaked past her, making her jump back in fright. She turned toward the door to see if anyone was there when the sound of a splash caught her attention. Gemma turned toward the bath, where water sloshed over the sides. A smug-looking Victor, the giant menace, popped up in between some bubbles. Gemma had no sooner recovered from the fright she'd gotten when Rhino barreled into the bathroom, his whole body twisting as his tail waved about. He gave her a little bark as if he was saying, 'watch this,' then hopped up the two tiled bath accessory steps. Standing on the opposite side of the tub to Gemma, she could've sworn she saw the little dog grin right before he belly-flopped into the bath.

A tidal wave of bathwater splashed over Gemma, drenching her. Victor growled and hissed at Rhino, who barked and tried to play with the annoyed cat. Victor, angry at having his bath disturbed, zapped Rhino with his sharp claws warning the dog he was not in the mood to play. Rhino ignored the spiteful cat, deciding to teach him a lesson in manners and pouncing on it. More water splashed over the tub's sides, and Victor's panicked screech echoed through the bathroom as Rhino sat down on the grumpy cat.

"Rhino," Gemma ignored her aching ribs and tried to push him off Victor, but the heavy dog wouldn't budge.

Gemma was finding it hard to balance on the wet floor. Knowing she would most likely regret her actions, Gemma climbed into the bath. Hoping she'd get a better grip on Rhino to push him off Victor before he drowned or was squashed. But as soon as Gemma was on her knees in the tub, a thrilled Rhino jumped up to welcome her to the fun. Finally free, Victor sprang into Gemma's arms, clinging to her to escape the over-exuberant dog. His sharp claws dug into Gemma's skin through her cotton shirt, raising red welts wherever his slashing paws got her. Gemma tried to pull him off her, but one of his claws got stuck in her cotton shirt, making the angry cat even angrier. Gemma freed Victor's claws and was about to get him out of the bath when Rhino decided he also wanted to be in Gemma's arms.

Barking excitedly, Rhino got ready to take a flying leap at Gemma, who was at the short end of the clawfooted tub. She stared in horror at the solid little dog ready to jump into her arms. Gemma knew if he hit her, she would end up with more than bruised ribs. Before Gemma could reprimand Rhino, he leaped towards her. Gemma quickly slid to one side, losing her grip on Victor, who slipped through her wet, soapy hands as Rhino flew past her like a white furry torpedo. At the same time, Victor used her face as a springboard to jump onto the marble countertop. He arced gracefully above Rhino, flying over the edge of the bath. Both animals hit their destinations almost simultaneously.

Rhino thumped to the ground, spinning, and skidding his way across the tiled floor towards the far wall. While above Rhino, Victor's graceful leap ended with him unable to stick the landing. The big cat splattered onto the marble countertop when his soapy paws slipped from under him. He spun and then peddled like crazy trying to stop his slippery, wet body from skidding down the marble countertop. But Victor's desperate attempts to slow down made him slide faster, and he slipped off the edge like a person losing control of the treadmill. Victor landed ungracefully on Rhino, who splayed out on the floor like a starfish.

"What is going on?" Gemma turned to see a stunned Dora staring at the scene before her.

Not wanting to stick around, Victor zipped out of the bathroom, encouraging Rhino to do the same, leaving Gemma kneeling in her clothes in the bath to take the fall for the mess. Gemma watched Dora's eyes travel over the wet floor to a soggy Gemma with puffs of evaporating bubbles hanging from her hair and face.

"My word, child," Dora stood staring at Gemma, her lips twitching as she bit her lip, trying not to laugh. "You look like you went a few rounds with a bubble monster."

"Try a crazy cat that tried to steal my bath, and an excitable bull terrier that doesn't want to get left out of the fun." Gemma threw her hands up and slid into the water, wondering if the day could get much crazier.

"Come on," Gemma heard Dora's voice from within her bubble fort and carefully sat up. She watched Dora dot the bathroom floor with towels which she walked over like she was crossing a pond by walking on Lily pads. "Let's get you out of the bath and dried off."

"I think I'm going to have a quick shower," Gemma told Dora while she helped her from the tub.

"Look at your arms," Dora tutted, examining the red welts on Gemma's arms and cheek. "That darn cat is a menace."

"I think he enjoys tormenting me." Gemma sloshed towards the shower and turned the water on.

"I've left your dinner on a warming tray in your room." Dora made sure enough towels were covering the wet floor. "Be careful you don't slip," she warned Gemma. "I'm going to say goodnight because Paul and I have our movie night tonight."

Gemma looked at her in surprise. Dora had gone from frosty to warm, and Gemma didn't know whether to be suspicious or just go with it. So, she decided to just go with it.

"What movie are you watching?" Gemma tested the water.

"I haven't asked," Dora said. "It's Paul's night to choose, so it will be some war movie or other, where things are being blown up." She shook her head. "But I have to watch because he watched what I choose."

"You remind me of my parents." Gemma felt her heart twinge and the sting of tears that always accompanied the feeling.

"I'm sorry about your parents," Dora touched Gemma's arms comfortingly.

"Thank you." Gemma cleared her throat and breathed away the tears.

"I'm going to leave you to have a shower," Dora said. "Before I go, I will check your room to make sure no critters are lurking around, and this time I will close your bedroom door." She walked to the bathroom door. "Molly will collect your dinner tray when you finish. Just put it outside your door and get a good night's sleep."

"I will," Gemma promised. "Good night, Dora. Enjoy movie night."

Dora said good night and left. Gemma checked the entire bathroom and then closed the bathroom door, deciding to lock it just to be sure. Victor was a cunning cat, and Gemma wouldn't be surprised if the feline knew how to open doors.

Chapter Three
A CAFÉ FULL OF MEMORIES

It was only seven-thirty p.m., Gemma had finished eating dinner, and Dora had popped back up half an hour ago to tend to Gemma's scratches. There was nothing on the television and she was feeling restless with flurries of anticipation, waiting for nine p.m. to arrive. And time seemed to be dragging, making every minute feel like an hour. She felt like a teenager sitting around counting the seconds to their first date. Gemma needed something to take her mind off whatever was going on inside her.

She stood up and looked out the large balcony doors. It was still light outside, and Gemma hadn't had the chance to properly explore the grounds of Honey Bay. She was dying to see the café. Besides, she knew that you needed to move around when you had bruised ribs to improve breathing and clear the lungs in case of mucus. Gemma looked at her t-shirt and calf-length cut-off jeans, wondering if she needed to take a sweater. The weather cooled down during the night and was turned a little chillier by the cool breeze that swept off the Atlantic.

Gemma grabbed a light sweater, just in case, and wrapped it around her waist, slipped on her sneakers, and headed for one of the doors downstairs that lead out towards the beach. After finding a door with a key in it and wondering what the heck was up with missing keys, Gemma slipped outside and stopped sucking in a breath at the view.

The sun was starting to dip towards the horizon, making its way to the other half of the world. It cast splashes of pink, orange, and gold across the sky, making the sea glitter and shimmer as if it was carpeted with diamonds and stars. The fresh sea air filled her lungs with its salty tang, gently humming in the distance and dancing along the shore. It was still warm out, and the gust of wind that touched her made gooseflesh pop up over her skin.

Dragging her eyes from the mesmerizing view of the ocean, Gemma made her way across the long rolling lawn. She walked down the slight slope toward the beach. Gemma wanted to stroll along in the sand to the café, but she didn't want her sneakers to be filled with it, so she walked along the grass verge that marked the perimeter between the two. She stood looking at the sea for a moment more, and as she was about to turn, she heard the jolly bark of Rhino, who had been scarce since the bath episode.

Gemma couldn't help but smile as she watched his short, stocky legs working hard as he ran full speed towards her. She bent down and patted him when he reached her.

"Hello, you," Gemma greeted Rhino. "I hope you came to apologize for your antics in the bath earlier?" She laughed, getting soggy doggy kisses over her face. "Apology accepted. But just so you know, I don't think you should be hanging around that Victor. He's a bad influence." Rhino gave a bark as if he agreed. "I'm glad you agree. Now let's go explore the café."

Gemma and Rhino continued along the path she was taking to the café until it came into view. Gemma stopped a distance away from it. Her heart thumped, and a feeling she could only describe as dreaded excitement welled up inside her while her feet froze to the ground. Gemma suddenly felt like she was staring into dark woods with no flashlight, having been warned there were monsters hidden and lurking behind every tree. The cautious part of Gemma, who had been missing these past few days, was back and warning her to turn and go back to the manor. While the more reckless Gemma wanted to throw caution to the wind and sate her morbid curiosity.

Gemma stood staring at the café perched on the edge of the grass that dipped down to the sand. It looked out over the sea with a wooden deck that wrapped part way around the side of the building before jutting out above the sand supported by tall wooden beams. From where Gemma stood, she could only see the side of the cafe and the two high windows looking at her like square eyes. She debated which part of herself to listen to when Rhino took the decision out of her hands. His ears stuck up straight, and his face pointed toward the café. He growled, barked, and then dashed forward, barking angrily as he ran to the stairs that led up onto the deck.

"Rhino!" Gemma shouted, fear prickling through her at Rhino's aggressive, angry barks. "Rhino!" She yelled louder. "Come back here." But he didn't listen, she saw him run up the steps on the side of the deck and then disappear into the café. "Bad dog!" She said through gritted teeth and started marching after him ignoring the warning alarm ringing in her head. "After the way she locked down the manor, why on earth would Dora leave the cafe door open?"

"This is a bad idea, Gemma," Gemma said through gritted teeth, picking up the pace when his barking got more intense. "If that's not Dora inside there..." She swallowed down the thought and kept marching.

When she was nearly at the door, she heard shuffling, and Rhino's barking stopped. Gemma was near the rickety stairs leading onto the deck that looked like they hadn't been used in years when she heard a bang and Rhino yelp. Gemma was about to rush up the deck stairs to find him but stopped when she heard a voice talking to the dog. Gemma moved around the side of the café to keep herself hidden and listened. She could hear shuffling, and the distinct knocking noise of Rhino's tail wagging against something — There was someone in there.

Gemma didn't know what to do. Should she approach and demand to know what the person was doing on private property? Or should she hightail it back to the house and get help?

"Get help or help Rhino," Gemma whispered out loud, weighing up what to do.

"I say we help Rhino," Dean's deep voice whispered in her ear, scaring Gemma, who was about to scream when his hand clamped over her mouth from behind. "Don't you dare bite me."

Gemma tried to talk, but his hand was over her mouth, so she pried it away, then turned to glare at him, "You scared half my life away!" She hissed at him in a whisper. "What were you thinking sneaking up on me like that?"

"That you were about to take on a vagrant by yourself, and luckily I saw you and Rhino wandering off when I got back from my aunt's," Dean whispered back.

Gemma felt she was standing too close to him when that weird tingly fluttery feeling swamped her system again, and she took a step back. Dean's eyes widened when he looked at her, and she knew he'd seen the angry red claw marks on her face. She lifted her hand to cover them, and he grabbed her arm, looking at it.

"What in the blazes happened to you?" He looked at her other arm and cheek.

"Victor," Gemma told him, pulling away. "But that's not important right now."

She swallowed and forced herself to concentrate on the problem at hand.

"That cat is a darn menace," Dean said, shaking his head, then turned and looked up at the window above them when another bang echoed from the café.

"Rhino!" A muffled voice came from inside, followed by a few barks, a growl, more crashing, and the sound of Rhino running.

Dean and Gemma looked at each other as they were about to run up the stairs when a huge rat-looking animal skidded to a halt on the top stairs. Its beady eyes scanned its escape route as Rhino came running up behind it. The rat decided to take the gap between Dean and Gemma. Only it missed and hit Gemma. She screamed, grabbed at it, and flung it onto the sand.

"I'm so tired of animals jumping on me!" Gemma hissed, shaking in disgust, and was nearly knocked off her feet by Rhino as he swooshed past them after the rat.

Dean stood staring at Gemma, startled by her outburst, and fighting to control the laughter she could see shimmering in his eyes.

"Don't you dare laugh!" Gemma warned him, her eyes narrowing angrily.

"I wouldn't dare!" Dean swallowed a few times and held up his hands.

Before either of them could say anything more, they heard the sound of footsteps on the far side of the deck. They both ran up that stairs and onto the deck but whoever was there had run down the stairs on the far side of the deck that led to the public car park over the border of Honey Bay Manor's property.

"Great, you scared them away!" Gemma blamed Dean, whose eyebrows rose in surprise as he looked at her.

"Me?" Dean asked, walking back up the deck and to the door of the café. "You're the one that screamed at that poor hutia."

"That what?" Gemma looked at him, confused.

"The hutia, the poor animal you flung ungraciously onto the sand," Dean reminded her.

"You mean the rat!" Gemma clarified.

"It's not a rat, but it is a rodent," Dean corrected her.

"That's what I said, a rat!" Gemma insisted.

"Not all rodents are rats," Dean told her, frowning as he looked at the broken lock on the door. "You wouldn't call porcupines, squirrels, beavers, and prairie dogs rats, would you?" He glanced at her. "Because they are also rodents."

"Whatever," Gemma huffed. "Can we forget about the..." She couldn't think of the name. "Rodent, and concentrate on the café?"

Dean pushed the door open and stepped in, but

as Gemma reached the threshold, she stopped. A cold shiver of fear slid up her spine, and she stepped back towards the deck. Dean turned to see why she hadn't joined him and frowned.

"Are you a vampire?" Dean teased her. "Is that why you can't cross the threshold?"

"I..." Gemma's eyes scanned the inside of the café, and images of her standing on the only bright yellow stool at the counter while dipping her finger in frosting popped into her head. "I need some air."

Gemma turned away from the café, hurrying along the empty, faded, and scarred deck that had some broken and rotting boards that she was careful to step around. But as Gemma walked along, her mind painted it with a gleaming reddish-brown, and scattered it with tables and chairs shaded by giant, brightly colored umbrellas. She stopped when she reached the railing at the end. Gemma turned to look at the empty space in front of her, where she knew two long wooden tables and benches once stood. As Gemma looked around the deck, images of how the empty space had once looked filled her mind. She turned and looked down below the deck. There had been a surf shack on the sand in front of the deck. It always smelled of scented wax and rubber wetsuits. Happy, beachy music always blared from the radio inside it. People would often dance in the sand when they gathered for sundowners on warm summer evenings.

"Gemma?" Dean's warm hand touched her shoulder, snapping her out of her thoughts, and the images vanished. "What's going on?" He asked her softly.

"I don't know," Gemma told him honestly, looking at him and trying to make sense of what she had seen. "But I think I've been here before."

"Earlier today, when I took you to the gazebo, you spaced out like a sleepwalker before you collapsed," Dean held her gaze. "The minute you looked into the café; I saw that same look on your face."

"You're going to think I'm crazy," Gemma's voice was soft.

"Try me," Dean said encouragingly.

"After I was released from hospital, after the accident, I started having bad nightmares. Every night the same one. One day I was planting flowers, and I had a flashback of me and someone I couldn't see, and whose voice I recognized but couldn't remember, burying a time capsule."

"I'm no doctor, but it sounds like suppressed memories." Dean looked around when Rhino dropped onto the deck and collapsed by their feet, exhausted from chasing the hutia.

"At first, it was just dreams about an accident I had when I was young," Gemma turned, leaned against the deck, staring out over the sea. "Then I got that letter from your uncle that included some pictures of the manor. One picture in particular triggered another flashback. That night the nightmare changed and became more vivid."

"What picture was it?" Dean asked her.

"The picture of the dock." Gemma turned to look in the direction of the dock, but she couldn't see it. She looked back at Dean in surprise. "What happened to it?"

"Gabby Marshall." Dean said, staring at Gemma like he was trying to climb into her mind. "She had it demolished the year her grandfather died." He drew the subject back to Gemma's nightmares and flashbacks. "Have your nightmares and flashbacks been stronger since you got to Honey Bay?"

Gemma looked at him and blinked in surprise, realizing she hadn't had a nightmare in two nights since she got to the island.

"I haven't had a nightmare since I arrived on the island." Gemma thought for a moment. "But I have had a lot of déjà vu, and earlier today..." She raised her eyebrows. "Well, you know what happened earlier today."

"I saw what happened, but you never told me what really happened," Dean pointed out. "And you haven't told me what happened a few minutes ago when you wouldn't walk into the café."

Gemma turned and looked at the café. The paint on the glass doors had long since peeled off, leaving them gray, brittle, and warped. The glass windows the door frames clung to were chipped, cracked, and covered with crusty salt residue from the sea air.

"I can see this place so clearly in my mind." Gemma stood away from the railing and walked to the middle of the deck. Rhino lay looking at her, then got up and went to stand by her side. "There were round tables that sat on the deck. The chairs were cast iron and padded with bright cushions and protective plastic covers." She turned, conjuring up the image. "There were big umbrellas with colorful patterns and heavy bases so they wouldn't move easily in the wind but could still be moved when needed." Gemma looked at Dean and smiled. "They stood shading the tables."

"I remember that." Dean breathed, looking at her in amazement.

"There were long wooden tables with benches only on one side that surrounded the railings. Three at each edge." She walked over to where Dean stood. "Down there, in front of the deck, was a wooden surf shop shack that my..." She frowned as she tried to remember but drew a blank. "I..."

She looked up at Dean, frustrated that the memory was stuck in her mind, and noticed he was staring at her like she'd grown two heads.

"You need to come with me," Dean said, grabbing her hand and pulling her towards the stairs.

"But what about the café and the vagrant?" Gemma was pulled behind him.

"True," Dean stopped and changed direction, not letting go of her hand. "Let me finish my check of the café, and then you need to come with me."

Gemma froze when they got closer to the door, "I can't!" She tugged on his hand, making him stop.

Dean nodded and let go of her hand, disappearing

inside the café. It wasn't long before he popped out carrying a chain and padlock, which he used to chain the cafe closed.

"That should secure it for the night," Dean said. "I'll come back in the morning and investigate."

"Why was there a chain in the café?" Gemma asked him, looking at the heavy object.

"To secure the door when there are heavy winds," Dean told her.

"I guess that makes sense." Gemma nodded.

"Now, can we go?" Dean looked at her with a raised eyebrow, and she nodded. "Good, because you will want to see what I have to show you."

Dean took her hand to lead her and Rhino back to the manor house, where he took her to the library. He left Gemma standing in the middle of the room with Rhino sitting at her feet as he navigated the sliding ladder that ran up the bookshelves. Dean found what he was looking for and climbed back down with a heavy book beneath his arm.

"Yesterday, when you told me that your father looked like Felix Marshall, I started doing a little digging," Dean told her, walking over to the desk in the corner of the room and setting down the leather-bound book. "I remembered my uncle telling me about a book in the Marshalls' library. I was going to look for it later today. But last night, after you told me about your déjà vu, I got the niggling feeling that I was overlooking something." Dean watched her walk over to him. "I couldn't sleep last night because that niggling feeling was hounding me, so I snuck into the house and found this."

"I've had that niggling feeling since I was a child," Gemma admitted. "I've always felt that there was something important I had forgotten."

"Yes, that feeling." Dean put his hand on the book. "But I have to warn you, though, that the information you're going to find may be a little shocking for you."

"What book is that?" Gemma asked, walking around the desk to stand next to him.

"The Marshall family tree, dating back forever," Dean told her.

Chapter Four

THE MARSHALL FAMILY TREE

"Oh wow!" Gemma breathed. Her eyes shone with excitement. "Is my father in it?"

"Do you know what Patricia Marshall's husband's name was?" Dean asked her instead of answering her.

"No, but I've heard everyone call him Doc," Gemma answered. "Everyone refers to her as Ms. Marshall, which I also find strange because she's married." She looked at Dean impatiently. "What has this got to do with my father?"

"Everything." Dean flipped through the pages of the book. "Patricia's father passed Honey Bay to her when he died. Patricia was a Marshall, not her husband." He stopped flipping through pages and looked at her. "There is a clause in Felix Marshall's will that has to be carried over to his direct descendant's wills. It states that only a direct descendant of Felix Marshall bearing the Marshall name can own Honey Bay."

"Patricia didn't take her husband's name." Gemma realized. That was one of Gemma's many questions answered. But it also left her with a whole lot more questions.

"Patricia was the first female Marshall to inherit Honey Bay since Felix was given the island in the mid eighteen hundreds," Dean told her. "Her attorney must've found a loophole allowing Patricia to keep the estate if she kept her last name.

Dean flipped the page, and Patricia Marshall was written in a calligraphic style at the top of the page. It had the date of her birth and her marriage listed below it, but Dean had his hand over who her husband was.

"Look at Patricia's husband's name," Dean lifted his hand, and Gemma's eyes widened.

"Doctor Jack Walker," she read and looked up at Dean. "My father must be related to Jack Walker!" Her brown creased in confusion. "But why would Patricia leave Honey Bay to my father? He's a Walker, not a Marshall."

Dean flipped the page to one with a new heading, and her jaw dropped. "Because I think your father is Patricia and Jack's only child."

Gemma stared down at the name on the page and started to feel lightheaded as the blood drained from her face when she saw the title — *Frederick Marshall,* calligraphed on the top of the page. Her mind vibrated with disbelief, and her eyes scanned the page.

"This couldn't be my father." She rubbed her forehead and leaned on the desk to steady herself. "It must be a coincidence that Patricia's son has the same name as my father," she muttered, but as much as she wanted to deny it, the birthdate was the same, and he was married to Wynonna Crane. Wynn Crane was what Gemma's father had called her mother. Questions tumbled through her mind looking at the life-changing evidence staring up at her. When another thought hit her, she turned to Dean "If Frederick Marshall is my father, then Gabby—"

"Would be your sister," Dean finished her thoughts for her.

"Are Gabby and I in the book?" Gemma felt her world start to unravel like a loose thread on a woolen sweater being pulled, slowly destroying the shape of the life she once knew.

Gemma turned the page, and a folded paper slipped out. Dean picked it up, but Gemma hardly noticed as the name at the top of the book's new page jumped out at her.

"Gemmima Marshall," Gemma read the name written in the same style as the other names in the book.

For a few seconds, Gemma thought, *"This isn't me, my name's not Gemmima, Dean has got it wrong, this is not me!"* But before her eyes drifted to the birthdate beneath the name, she knew she was Gemmima Marshall. She could feel it in her soul as a piece of something that had been missing inside her fell into place. But there were still so many pieces missing and parts that didn't make sense. Her mind whirled, trying to process it all.

"Gemma?" Dean's soft voice broke through the fog, clouding her mind. "Are you okay?"

Am I okay? Gemma thought and gave a soft laugh. "I've just discovered my entire life was built on a paper foundation laid over a mountain of secrets and half-truths. I feel like I've just fallen down a rabbit hole and landed in a strange world only to be told the strange, crazy world was the real one and the one I fell from was an illusion."

"I get it," Dean said. "I won't pretend to know exactly what you're going through. But I do know what it is like to have the only world you've ever known ripped away from you, leaving you stranded in a strange new place."

"Not only physically orphaned, but emotionally and mentally as well." Gemma swallowed down the burning lump in her throat.

Her emotions had been stretched to a breaking point. She looked at Dean. His blue eyes were filled with compassion and an understanding that only someone who'd had their world shattered would have.

"Gemma, I'm not a wizard. Although that would be cool, I can't make any of this easier or go away." He reached over and wiped a stray tear from her cheek, giving her a warm smile. "Heck, I can't promise I'll ever understand what you're going through. But if you let me." He took her hand, making her heart jump and tiny shocks zing up her arm. "I can help you sort through it and put the pieces together."

Gemma looked at Dean in surprise. His words floated into her heart and comforted her broken soul. While the walls of her world tumbled down around her and the paper foundation it was built on got ripped into shreds, he made her feel she had a rock to rest on while she caught her breath.

"Thank you, Dean." Gemma gave his hand a slight squeeze.

Rhino took that moment to decide he was bored and stood up, knocking into Dean, who dropped the folded paper he'd taken from the book.

"What is that?" Gemma watched Dean dip down to pick it up. "It was in between the pages."

"Yes." Dean looked at the paper in hand and held it out to her. "I'm not quite sure how to tell you this, so you should read it yourself."

"Tell me what?" Gemma's brow creased. She took the paper from Dean and unfolded it. Her brow bounced up as she read the document in her hand. "I died?" She looked at him blankly before blinking and looking at the death certificate he had handed to her. Another thought occurred to her, and she looked at Dean accusingly. "This is why you wanted to run my DNA. You wanted to make sure I was who I said I was."

"Yes, that was part of it," Dean admitted.

"What was the other part?" Gemma couldn't

believe she was looking at her death certificate. It was morbid and surreal.

"To prove that you are not Gabby Marshall," Dean confessed.

"You still don't believe I'm not Gabby?" Gemma was flabbergasted. "I don't believe you!" Her eyes narrowed. "I've just let you into my deepest secrets and trusted you with personal information I haven't even told my best friend. But you still don't trust me!"

"Can I explain?" Dean put his hands up in front of him.

"Go ahead." Gemma folded her arms in front of her chest.

"The day you arrived on the island was when I got the first message from Gabby," Dean explained. "So, naturally, when I saw you at the diner, it was a shock. Especially as Gabby had disappeared under mysterious circumstances."

"Which you still haven't told me about," Gemma pointed out.

"I will," Dean promised.

"So, you spilled your coffee on me and dumped your donut in my hair because of a message you thought Gabby sent you!" Gemma looked at him with raised eyebrows.

"To be fair," Dean held up his hand again. "You bumped into me."

"I was pushed into you by one of the rude patrons of the diner," Gemma corrected him.

"I didn't see anyone push you," Dean told her. "I turned around, and to me you were Gabby Marshall up to her usual destructive way of getting attention or what she wanted."

"What did she want?" Gemma's brow knitted together curiously.

"Her client file from my uncle." Dean's expression mirrored Gemma's.

"Do you know why?" Gemma looked at the family tree book.

"I asked. She wouldn't tell me," Dean answered. "That is when I discovered the missing client information. Only the general information was in the files listing their visits to my uncle, case numbers, etcetera." He rubbed his chin. "My uncle was a diligent record keeper. *To be prepared was to be pre-armed* was his motto, because surprises were what lost cases and got people into a lot of trouble or worse."

"He sounds like the kind of attorney everyone wants to have," Gemma commented. "I wonder what he had that Gabby wants badly enough to burn down his house for."

"Probably the same information she was accused of burning down the police station for." Dean looked at the book.

"I thought you said she didn't burn it down?" Gemma reminded him.

"The charges were dropped because of her alibi," Dean said, and his eyes flashed anger. "When it comes to Gabby Marshall, you can't really trust anything she says or does because there is always an ulterior motive behind her actions."

"Why do you dislike her so much?" Gemma wanted to know.

"She is always getting my cousin into trouble and has done so since they were kids," Dean told Gemma. "My cousin has been in love with her for longer than I remember. Even after everything she has done to him, he still stands by her and loves her."

"What did she do to Garrett?" Gemma was curious to know.

"The better question would be, what hasn't she done to him," Dean shook his head. "This last disappearance, I hoped Garrett would finally see sense, but instead, he's determined to find her." He gave a snort. "Gabby went to see Garrett at work on the night she disappeared. She told Garrett that she finally found the proof she needed that her mother never committed suicide."

"Gabby really was obsessed with that, wasn't she?" Gemma blew out a breath and shook her head.

"You have no idea." Dean ran a hand through his hair. "Garrett was tired of Gabby's obsession with her mother's death, especially when her grandmother had just died. Garrett and Patricia were very close. Garrett was also tired of Gabby coming and going as she pleased while he waited for her. They had the usual fight about Gabby growing up and Garrett wanting to start a family."

"They sound like a perfect couple," Gemma said sarcastically.

"Garrett stormed out of his off with his last words to Gabby being that he wanted a divorce because if they stayed together any longer, he may just end up killing her." Dean's jaw clenched. "Gabby was left in Garrett's office, and she immediately called me to give me an earful. I was still in Miami, ready to move back to Honey Bay. She told me I should think twice before coming back here because the island isn't big enough for both of us." A muscle ticked at the side of his mouth. "I reminded her that she no longer owned the entire island and wouldn't even have the manor or fruit orchard to lord over for much longer."

"That wasn't very nice of you," Gemma told him.

"Gabby and I have said worse to each other," Dean assured Gemma with a flash of anger in his now stormy blue eyes. "That's when she sneered about how she'd never cared about Honey Bay, a little rock in the middle of nowhere, and went on to rub it in how easily she could dismantle Honey Bay piece by piece, with the change of her last name, whenever she wanted to."

Gemma could see how badly Gabby had riled him that day when his fists clenched at his sides.

"She really gets to you, doesn't she?" Gemma touched his arm, her heart instantly doing an excited bounce when he covered her hand with his. "What happened after that?"

"Garrett had a signed baseball bat in his office

from his favorite player," Dean told Gemma. "Garrett's assistant heard Gabby arguing with me on the phone and thought she was talking to Garrett. She hadn't seen him leave the office."

"I think I can see where this is going." Gemma let her hand drop, and Dean took it in his.

"The assistant had to go and deliver wages in the factory and left not wanting to disturb an argument between her boss and a Marshall." Dean drew in a breath. "About half an hour after Garrett left to cool off, he went back to his office, and it looked like a tornado had gone through it."

"Did Gabby wreck Garrett's office with his baseball bat?" Gemma's eyes were huge with disbelief.

"We don't know what happened there." Dean blew out a breath. "You should see the crime scene photos." He shook his head. "Garrett didn't know what to think, but he saw his baseball bat lying on the floor and picked it up, only to find blood on the handle and top of the bat. Blood that turned out to be Gabby's."

"Oh no!" Gemma's face fell, knowing why Garrett was in so much trouble without Dean telling her.

"So, you can imagine what happened next." Dean looked down at their linked hands. "That night, Gabby didn't go home. She wasn't at the manor, and no one had seen her since Garrett's office. Garrett had to report the damage to his office to claim on insurance for some of the broken furniture. The new police captain personally presided over the case, and as soon as he found out there was blood on the baseball bat, he opened a case."

"With Garrett as his number one suspect," Gemma guessed, and Dean nodded.

"The dog unit tracked Gabby's trail of blood down to Fruit Island docks where Garrett's yacht was missing," Dean told her. "But they couldn't find the yacht or Gabby. Three weeks after Gabby disappeared, my cousin's house got broken into, and someone tried to strangle him. They were looking for the information Gabby had."

"Maybe she does have evidence about her mother?" Gemma suggested.

"I think that is what my uncle thought," Dean told her. "The man he went to meet the day before he came to visit me in Miami was helping my uncle with some investigation. He isn't the bad guy the police think he is. His kid died of an overdose, and now he is trying to clean up the streets but from the inside."

"Pity it took a tragedy like that for him to change sides." Gemma's eyes narrowed, and anger spurted through her. "I have seen the ravages of drugs."

"The man also has his ear to the ground about a lot of other things. He owes my uncle his life and would never have sabotaged his car," Dean said. "The man supposedly gave my uncle some crucial information about Gabby and her family. I think that is the information Gabby wants."

"By 'her family,' you mean me?" Gemma looked at him.

"I'm not sure, because I haven't seen what it is," Dean admitted. "That is why I was so eager to find my uncle's files."

"Speaking of your uncle," Gemma had noticed the minute she'd walked into the library that Dean had put his uncle's butler's table in the room "I see you found a new home for your uncle's table?"

"I put it there because I have no space in the cottage," Dean told her. "I hope you don't mind?"

"Well, I don't have a lot of space in this house, you know," Gemma teased him. "Of course, I don't mind."

Gemma reluctantly let go of Dean's hand, walked over to the desk, and ran her hand over it. "My father had one of these when I was about eight or nine, and it looked like this one."

Dean frowned and walked over to her, "This was in your grandfather's clinic," he reminded her.

Gemma looked at him wide-eyed and blinked in surprise, "You don't think this is the same table?"

"How would we know?" Dean asked.

"Because I used to play with it all the time." Gemma pulled up a clip on the side and lifted the flat top of the table, showing Dean the box tray section of the table. "This one has the lid to cover the plates with. The one my father had was designed for a young lady in love with one of the kitchen workers. She had it made with a trick bottom so they could leave love letters to each other."

"Crafty," Dean said, watching her.

"I wrote my own love letter on the..." She put her finger into what looked like nothing more than a notch on the bottom of the box tray' section of the wood and pulled. The bottom of the tray lifted out. She flipped it over and stared at what was stuck to the bottom of it. "Dean..."

"That's a flash drive." Dean reached down and pulled the tape off it, looking at Gemma in disbelief.

Chapter Five
LOCKED DOORS

"I take it this isn't what you left on the lid?" Dean held it up.

"No, mine is the sharpie artwork." Gemma pointed to her drawing that was on the lid in amazement.

There was a picture of three stick figure girls with their names written in a childish scrawl, Terri, Gemma, and Dee.

"Nice drawing," Dean commented.

"I was about six or seven," Gemma told him.

"Who is Dee?" He looked at her curiously. "I know you've spoken about Terri."

Gemma felt her cheeks heat, "You're going to laugh."

"Was she your doll?" Dean guessed.

"No, my imaginary friend." Gemma laughed nervously. Only Terri had known about Dee. "She saved me." Gemma had no idea why she blurted that out.

"How did your imaginary friend save you?" Dean looked at her, intrigued.

"It doesn't matter," Gemma said, moving the conversation in another direction. "If that drive was in your uncle's house, it could mean that he moved all his paper files onto it."

"That is what I was thinking." Dean looked around the room. "Do you have a laptop?"

"I do," Gemma told him. "It's upstairs."

"Mine is at the office." Dean looked at the flash disk and handed it to her. "Why don't you hold onto this, and we can have breakfast together tomorrow morning to go through it?"

"Is that your way of inviting yourself to breakfast?" Gemma looked at him with raised brows.

"I'm so sick of cereal," Dean admitted. "I'm dying for one of my grandmother's cooked breakfasts." He looked at her with big soulful eyes.

"Fine, we can do that." Gemma laughed. "Now, can we look at Gabby's page in the Marshalls' book?"

They walked back to the Marshall family tree book, and Gemma turned the page to see 'Gabriela Marshall' written.

"Oh, I nearly forgot," Dean said. "Congratulations. You have a twin sister."

Gemma stared at Gabby's birthdate in shock.

"My parents left half of their estate to her,"

Gemma said and looked at Dean. "But her name is wrong in the will. Can you help me with that?"

"Help you get her cut from your parent's will?" Dean looked hopeful.

"Don't be like that!" Gemma shook her head at him. "She has a right to her father's estate as much as I do."

"Yes, but it's going to be tricky sorting out the Marshall estate now that we know she is alive," Dean said softly. "Although you are the eldest living, Marshall."

"It's only fair that everything is equally divided," Gemma said. "After all, this is her home. I didn't grow up here."

"Neither did Gabby. She was at boarding school most of her young life," Dean reminded her. "But when we find her and she sorts the mess she put Garretts in, and we find what is in those files, I will look into what can be done."

"Thank you, Dean," Gemma said, then became thoughtful. "How would Gabby changing her surname dismantle the island?" Gemma asked.

"Gabby is also a Walker and could change her name to her father's if she wanted to," Dean told her, "Which would mean that the entire island would revert back to the original owner."

"That's a bit drastic, isn't it?" Gemma argued. "I mean, once you've inherited something, it becomes yours, and you can make up the rules. What has a last name got to do with anything?"

"Every Marshall who has had Honey Bay has included that stipulation in their will," Dean told her. "Because it has something to do with the deed of Honey Bay Island."

"The deed?" Gemma looked confused.

"Honey Bay was first owned by a wealthy merchant ship owner," Dean explained. "It was given to Felix Marshall as a reward for saving the man's daughter from pirates. Felix also recovered the treasure the pirates had stolen from the merchant's ship that had been attacked."

"So, Felix was a hero?" Gemma commented.

"Felix was the commanding officer of a naval ship that patrolled these waters." Dean's eyes lit up as he told the story. "He was sailing back to port after his ship was damaged by another battle. He had also lost most of his crew. But still, he helped stop the attack of the merchant's ship, sank the pirate's ship, and rescued the merchant's daughter." Dean said with pride. "Felix was my hero when I was a kid."

"I can see that," Gemma said. "So, the merchant gave Felix Honey Bay Island?" She frowned. "Why this island?"

"Felix asked for it," Dean answered Gemma's first question. "The pirate attack on the merchant's happened just off the shore of Honey Bay. The wreckage of the pirate ship is a diving attraction for the island."

"So why was Felix the only one to get an island?" Gemma asked. "What about his men?"

"He didn't have a lot of men at the beginning of the skirmish, and only three besides Felix survived the pirate skirmish but were badly wounded," Dean told her. "Three pirates had loaded treasure onto their rowing boats and headed for the shore, taking the merchant's daughter hostage."

"I take it Felix took a rowboat and headed after the pirates to rescue her and the treasure?" Gemma took a guess.

"Yes, single-handedly." Dean stared at the book, remembering the story. "Felix rowed ashore after the pirate where he killed all three of them, rescued the merchant's daughter, and saved the treasure."

"For his reward, the man gave him Honey Bay and Fruit Island," Gemma guessed incredulously.

"Correct," Dean confirmed.

"And no one thought to question that story?" Gemma asked. "It doesn't seem real that Felix took on three armed pirates. And if there were three-row boats filled with treasure, how would he have got it all back to the ship on his own?"

"It's a gallant and true story," Dean looked offended by her questioning the history of the island he was born on and the integrity of his hero.

"Yes, but it just seems off," Gemma said skeptically.

"Regardless of your skepticism," Dean said. "The merchant gifted the island to Felix for as long as a direct descendant of Felix lived on Honey Bay and bore his name, the island would remain the home and property of the Marshalls."

"That's not much of a gift," Gemma pointed out. "It's more like a long-term lease expiring when the Marshall line, in particular from Felix's line, comes to an end."

"That's what Felix agreed to, and it's never been changed or challenged," Dean told her, a little stiffly, obviously annoyed that Gemma had dared to challenge his hero.

"You really love that story, don't you?" Gemma grinned.

"What's not to love? It's full of pirates, treasure, and damsels in distress." Dean's eyes sparkled.

Gemma looked down at the book and saw the death certificate lying next to it.

"What about this?" Gemma asked, moving the conversation away from Felix Marshall, who Gemma had some serious doubts about. "I'm sure this nulls my inheritance."

"I will find out if it's fakey," Dean promised, taking the document, and slipping it into his jeans pocket. "Speaking of the inheritance, we need to have a conversation sometime soon about it. We need to discuss something before ownership becomes yours, and it is quite urgent."

"Okay." Gemma gave Dean a sideways glance. "Do you want to discuss it now?"

"No, it can wait until the morning," Dean told her.

"So, what do we do now?" Gemma asked him, not wanting the evening to end.

"Now..." Dean grinned. "We've gone down the rabbit hole. Let's go have a party."

"What did you have in mind?" Gemma watched Dean dig a bunch of keys from his jacket pocket.

"How about we go explore those locked rooms upstairs?" Dean rattled the keys.

"You know I'm dying to get into them," Gemma said excitedly. "But I think we should put the book back first."

Dean nodded and put the book back before they headed up the stairs, where they were joined by a happy Rhino trotting behind them to the top landing.

"Where do you want to start?" Dean stood looking at the locked doors of the east wing.

"On the third floor," Gemma told him. "If my father was Patricia and Jack's son, his suite is on the third floor." She looked at Dean. "Now that I know who I am, I want to know why my father took me away and never told me about our family in Honey Bay. Because there must be a reason that he'd fake a death certificate for one daughter and leave his other one with his parents." She had to believe her father had a good reason to do what he had done. "Especially only a year after their mother died."

"Why do you think it was your father who faked your death certificate?" Dean asked her.

"Because the death certificate is from Miami."

Gemma turned to walk towards the stairs. "Remember I told you I had a bad accident when I was six?"

"I don't think you told me your age," Dean said. "But yes, I do."

"I was taken to a hospital in Miami," Gemma told him. "I was there for many weeks with a bad head injury, and my ankle was badly broken. It took a long time to heal."

"I will find out what I can," Dean patted the pocket with the death certificate in as he followed Gemma up the small staircase to the third-floor landing.

The landing opened into a wide space with a sofa and a few chairs that were covered with sheets in front of a large window that looked out over the front gardens of the manor house. Through it, they could see the evening taking over from the daylight. Eerie shadows were being cast through the speckled silver threads of dust particles trickling gently through the air. Gemma could imagine how beautiful it must be to sit up here on a clear evening when the stars came out, adorned in jeweled evening wear.

"What a beautiful space," Gemma said, looking around the room and trying to get a feel from it like she had with the rest of the house, but there was nothing. "I don't recognize this room."

"Let's explore through one of the four doors surrounding us." Dean pointed to the double doors on their right, then the ones on the left, before pointing to the two single entries in the middle, numbering them door one, door two, door three, and door four. "Which will it be?"

"Why are there only four doors up here?" Gemma tilted her head. "This floor must run the entire length of the manor." She looked around the third-floor landing.

"Let's start with the two smaller doors in front of us," Dean suggested. "I feel the double doors will take a little longer."

"Good idea," Gemma agreed, following Dean to the first door, where it took him four tries to find the key. "We need something to mark the keys with."

"I only have so many pockets," Dean pointed out, pushing the door open.

Gemma stepped into a room that was a smaller version of the rooms she was in, but there were no balcony doors, only large windows running along the wall's far side. The room had a small walk-in closet next to a bathroom. The furniture, as on the landing, was covered with bedsheets. Not finding anything, they left the room, carefully locking the door behind them. Dora was just warming up to Gemma and she didn't want to fall back onto her frosty side.

The room next to the first one was a mirror image of the previous room.

"That was disappointing," Gemma said, waiting for Dean to lock the door.

"Are you sure my grandmother said this was Patricia's son's suite?" Dean asked her.

"She did," Gemma confirmed.

"This whole floor was his suite?" Dean looked amazed, walking with Gemma to the double doors on the right of the landing, finding the key on the second try. "I feel like a game show host about to open up a grand prize through magic doors."

"Well, go on then," Gemma encouraged. "Let's see what's behind door number three."

Dean swept the double doors open and stood staring inside. The room ran the length of the east wing below it. The first door on the left was a study with big windows overlooking the sea. There was a door that led from the study into a full bathroom. Another door led to the hallway and one that led into the huge bedroom. As you came out of the bathroom, there was a dressing room on the right.

Once again, all the furnishings were covered. The king-sized bed sat in the middle of the room with double doors on either side leading out onto balconies. Gemma could picture pretty patio furniture on each for catching the afternoon sun. The door on the right-hand side of the hallway mirrored the one on the left. There was another dressing room and a full bathroom, but instead of a study, there was a small art studio.

Dean walked over to a covered painting on an easel in the art studio and pulled it off, turning around as Gemma gasped when she saw the picture. She stared at the portrait of two identical little girls with bouncy chestnut curls sitting on the deck of

Honey Bay café beneath a bright blue sky. Their image was beautiful and resonated with warmth and happiness. At the same time, there was a haunting sadness in the background. In the sky, a lone bird sailed near the sun, and peeping out of the trees off to the one side of the cafe was a deer with sad eyes.

"That's you and Gabby." Dean managed to tell them apart. And Gemma knew he'd done so because of the scar on Gabby's forearm. He looked at Gemma worriedly. "Did you have another vision or déjà vu feeling?"

Gemma shook her head, "I wasn't shocked because of a vision. It's because I never called her Gabby." Gemma swallowed, confused, and tried to conjure up the memory she needed. But there was nothing but a blank wall.

"What did you call her?" Dean frowned curiously.

"Dee!" Gemma breathed, feeling a familiar pressure in her head.

Her knees wobbled as her body turned to jelly when the flashback hit her. Pain pierced her eyes, forcing them to shut when she heard Dean call her name. Gemma felt herself sway, and as her knees buckled, a pair of warm, strong arms wrapped around her as she was pulled back in time.

Chapter Six

THE GOLD COINS

TWENTY-NINE YEARS AGO

Gemma and Dee were playing on the stairs of Honey Bay Café while they waited for their grandmother to close for the evening. It was Gemma and Dee's birthday in four days, and Gemma had found a present for them. She'd found it while exploring in a garden when their father had taken them with him to work for the day. Gemma loved collecting interesting rocks or pieces of glass from the sand. Earlier that day, she found two weird coins with exciting patterns on them. After picking them up, she thought they were magic lucky coins left for her and Dee's birthday by the fairies living in Honey Bay's gardens.

"I found us a birthday present," Gemma whispered to Dee. "But you can't tell anyone because they are magic lucky coins."

"Let me see," Dee said excitedly as Gemma pulled them out of her pocket. "Wow!"

Dee picked up one of the coins and stared at it.

"You must put it in your pocket and carry it with you forever," Gemma instructed.

"They will keep us connected forever," Dee said, giving Gemma a hug. "I will love it always and always and always."

"Hello, girls," Gemma felt her skin crawl as she turned around to see the bad lady grinning down at them. "What are you two up to today?"

"Nothing!" Dee said cheekily.

Gemma slipped her coin into her pocket and took her sister's hand before she got into trouble with all her sass. When Dee didn't like someone, she wasn't afraid to tell them. And they did not like the bad lady.

"We're waiting for Grandmother," Gemma said politely.

"Is she still here?" The bad lady asked.

"No, she's at the store!" Dee rolled her eyes.

"Still as cheeky as always, little—" She glanced down at the wrists to see which color band they each wore to know which twin she was talking to. "Gabby."

"You're very ru..." Before Dee could say any more, Gemma, who was looking forward to their birthday party, pulled Dee up to take her into the café.

But Gemma hadn't stuck her coin in her pocket correctly and it fell out before bouncing down the stairs.

"Gemma, your magic lucky coin!" Dee shouted and went after it.

"What's this?" The bad lady bent down and scooped it up before Dee could get to it.

"Give it back!" Dee shouted at her.

Gemma saw the bad lady look at the coin, rub it, and then bite it.

"What are you doing?" Gemma said rudely, jumping up to try and snatch her magic lucky coin back.

"Where did you get this?" The bad lady bent down low and shoved the coin in Gemma's face.

"That's none of your business," Gemma knew she was being rude to an adult, but the bad lady was mean and nasty to them all the time.

The bad lady grabbed Gemma by the arm, yanking Gemma towards her. Her evil eyes bore into Gemma, while she squeezed Gemma's arm painfully.

"Tell me where you got this from, you little brat!" The bad lady said through clenched teeth.

"Leave my sister alone," Dee shouted, jumping off the stairs and springing at the woman to get her to release Gemma's arm. The woman pushed Dee, who went flying and fell back against the deck stairs, screaming in pain. Gemma felt bile rise when she heard a snap like someone standing on a twig.

"What is going on out here?" They heard their grandmother's voice.

The bad lady let Gemma go, pocketed the coin, and quickly dashed towards Dee.

"Oh, my goodness, Gabby, I told you not to swing on the railing," the bad lady lied.

"Dee!" Gemma shouted and ran to her sister, lying sobbing at the base of the stairs holding her broken arm. "It's okay." Gemma sat down next to her sister, holding her, and stroking her hair while their grandmother called the ambulance. "You're a hero, and you saved me." She kissed her sister's head, tears rolled down Gemma's cheeks, and a pain slashed her heart. Her sister had saved her. It was because of Gemma that Dee was hurt. Gemma vowed that no one would hurt her little sister again. She owed Dee her life for saving her from the bad lady.

"Gemma!" Dean sat on the art studio floor, cradling Gemma's limp body in his lap. Her face was so pale. "Please, Gemma, wake up."

Dean moved a lock of shiny chestnut hair from her face. He didn't know what to do. He needed to get her some water but couldn't leave her lying on the floor. He had to try and stand up so he could take her and lay her on a bed or a sofa. Dean was carefully slipping her off him so he could stand when she started to moan.

"Dee!" Gemma's eyes flew open, nearly scaring Dean to death and then knocking him out when she shot up and her head connected with his chin. "Ow!" She grunted and grabbed her ribs, looking around her, confused for a second, blinking, and then looking at Dean.

Dean rubbed his painful chin, "Welcome back." He looked at her with a smile. "I wondered when you'd rejoin me because my leg has gone numb."

"What?" Gemma's brows creased, then her eyes widened when she realized they were on the floor, and she was cradled in his lap. "Oh, no!" She said, scrambling to her feet, swaying as she got her balance, and then wincing because she moved too quickly. "I'm sorry, Dean."

"Don't be sorry," Dean said. "Now that I know about your flashbacks, I can help you."

Gemma stared at him for a minute. She had a look of uncertainty in her eyes and looked like she wanted to bolt. But instead, she sighed and smiled, a smile that lit up her soulful brown eyes and stole his breath away, making his heart pound in his chest. Dean swallowed a few times as their eyes met and held. He had to fight the urge to pull her to him and kiss her, and he gave himself a mental shake.

You are definitely not ready to go down the relationship route! He admonished himself. Dean had just gotten a very long and messy divorce after a bitter two-year battle with his ex-wife. He most certainly couldn't afford to fall for the alluring Doctor Gemma Walker. No matter how beautiful her smile, how soft her brown eyes, or how shiny her chestnut hair was.

Good grief, man! Get a grip. As soon as Gemma has found what she's looking for and finalized the estate, she'll return to her fancy life in L.A. He gave himself a good dose of reality, cleared his throat, and broke eye contact when he realized he was still staring at her.

"I think we've had enough for one night," Dean said, hoping she overlooked the slight gruffness of his voice or the way his hand shook when he locked the double doors once they'd left the master suite.

"When can we do the rest of the house?" Gemma asked.

"I'll see if I can get a sitter for Sophie tomorrow night," Dean said. "If you don't have any plans, that is."

"Let me see," Gemma said teasingly, "Other than dinner with a prince, I'm free."

"Good, then it's a date," the word slipped out of his mouth for the second time that day.

"Great," Gemma surprised him by saying and looked at her wristwatch, surprised to see it was only ten-thirty. "Would you like to get some hot chocolate before you go?"

"Sure," Dean said, not wanting the evening to end, and followed her back down to the ground floor and then through to the kitchen. Where he noticed her staring at the cupboards. "Do you even know your way around this kitchen?"

"No," Gemma admitted.

"That's why you asked me to stay for hot chocolate," Dean teased her. "Because you don't know where anything is."

"Guilty," Gemma laughed.

"Then let me give you a quick lesson," Dean said.

They sat at the kitchen table a few minutes later, sipping hot chocolate.

"Do you want to tell me where you went when you passed out?" Dean asked her.

Gemma blew out a breath and, to his surprise, told him about the flashback she'd had.

Dean stared at her in amazement for a minute when she'd finished telling him about what she'd seen while in the art studio.

"So now you know how Gabby got that nasty scar on her wrist," Gemma finished her story. "It was my fault."

"How was that your fault?" Dean put his cup down and leaned on the table.

"I was the one who took the coins and started the fight with whoever that woman was that we called the bad lady," Gemma shuddered. "I can't for the life of me remember her face. Even when I see her in my flashbacks or dreams, I look right at her but don't see her."

"Try not to force it," Dean said, feeling stupid because he had no idea what to tell or do for her.

He made a mental note to research this type of trauma. He couldn't speak to his grandmother or Barney for advice because he'd promised Gemma to keep her episodes between them. Dean had just started to earn her trust, and he didn't want to break the thin thread of trust they were weaving between them.

"About Sophie," Gemma turned the conversation around. "Why don't you bring her with you tomorrow night?"

"Are you sure?" Dean looked at her in surprise.

"Of course," Gemma said. "I'm sure she wants to spend time with her dad, and I would like to see her again. We had a delightful conversation the first night I arrived at the manor."

"I'm sure she'd enjoy that," Dad said. "She has been asking me when she can come visit you since that night."

"Why don't we get whatever take-out is her favorite," Gemma suggested. "And make an evening out of exploring the manor."

"As long as my grandmother doesn't find out that I got the keys from Sully," Dean said in a low voice.

"Who's Sully?" Gemma asked. "And why would he have the door keys in the manor?"

"He is the local locksmith in town who Doc used to make spares of all the keys for the manor and his clinic," Dean explained. "He also owns the store where you were nearly run down."

"That's where you disappeared when I couldn't find you at the store?" Gemma realized.

"Yes, Sully was getting me the keys for the manor," Dean confirmed.

"Thank you, Dean," Gemma's voice dropped, and her eyes met his. "I had an eventful day, and I even had a bubble bath fight with Victor and Rhino."

Gemma told Dean what happened in the bathroom, and he couldn't remember when last he'd had such a good laugh. His eyes fell on the welt on her cheek, and all he wanted to do was kiss it better, and then he gave himself another stern talking.

"Where is Sophie's mother?" Gemma asked Dean after he told her how the only person Victor has liked since Patricia died is Sophie.

"We separated four years ago when Sophie was five," Dean told Gemma, surprising himself by finding he wanted to tell Gemma. "She was never much of a mother. My ex is on the fast track to making a partnership at a big law firm in Miami. When we first got married, she was so different. Then she fell pregnant, and I saw who she really was. When Sophie was two, Angela, my ex, joined the firm she's with now, and we stuck it out together for another three years of fighting. Which wasn't good for Sophie, who lived with her mother but didn't really know her. I was the one who got her ready for school, packed her lunch, made all her meals, took her to parties, got her play costumes made."

"I'm sorry, Dean," Gemma said, reaching over the

table and taking his hand to give it a supportive squeeze.

"When Sophie was five, Angela walked out on us without so much as a backward glance or a goodbye to Sophie," Dean felt the anger rise in his stomach. "When I filed for divorce, she got even meaner. She wanted everything and used Sophie as the tool to get it."

"Everything?" Gemma asked.

"Yes, my parents left me some money when they died," Dean told her. "My uncle invested it and made me a nice nest egg. Luckily, he also made Angela sign a prenup so she could never get her hands on that nest egg for Sophie's future."

"But she got the house?" Gemma guessed.

"Yes, she got the beachfront house we bought after we got married," Dean told her. "Plus, all the furniture because she said she'd handpicked each item."

"What a cow," Gemma said, shaking her head. "Sorry!"

"No, you're right. She is a cow." Dean laughed. "It was just a house and some furniture. But she also took two years to decide what she wanted and dangled Sophie in front of me like she was nothing more than a pawn in Angela's game." He ran a hand through his hair. "A month before Sophie's birthday this year, we had a conversation and agreed we would move back to Honey Bay. Sophie loves it here, so it didn't take much convincing."

"We moved into the cottage that Patricia gave me when I turned nineteen," Dean told her. "She said it was my home and would always be there for me to go to."

"Oh, that's lovely." Gemma smiled that smile that made his heart thump and stole the breath from him.

Dean didn't want the evening to end. After he told Gemma about Angela, they talked about her life in L.A. and the accident.

"I'm so sorry about your parents, Gemma," Dean said again. "I know it's so cliché, but the ache dulls over time. But to be honest, it never goes away. I still miss my parents and get heartsore when I think of them."

"Since I've been here, I've felt like I can finally start healing," Gemma said and looked down at her hands. Her eyes clouded over, and he saw her struggling with something. "I feel calmer and not anxious like I'm supposed to be somewhere because here I feel I'm already where I need to be." She looked up and gave him a small smile. "Does that sound crazy?"

"Not at all," Dean assured her. "Honey Bay is part of you, it's where you were born. I could never wait to return to Honey Bay when traveling with my parents. It was a relief when I let go of Miami to come home. Like you, I also felt out of place. Here I'm home." He looked at her. "If you decide to stay, the island needs a new doctor, and Doc has got quite a clinic."

"That is tempting," Gemma told him, and a

shadow passed over her eyes again. "But I'm afraid I wouldn't be any good as a doctor."

"But you're a surgeon!" Dean frowned.

"A surgeon who has developed an aversion to blood and looking at, what Terri calls, gore," Gemma confessed and told Dean what happened on her first day back at work after the accident. "I get full-blown panic attacks."

Dean was about to say something when they heard a thump from the hallway. They looked at each other, and both stood up quietly. Dean put his finger over his lips, and keeping her behind him, they made their way into the entry hall, where they saw Victor sitting on the table next to the entry hall.

Dean sighed in relief. He looked at his wristwatch and was surprised to see it was almost midnight.

"It's late," Dean said. "I'd better call it a night."

"I had a great night," Gemma told him.

"I did too." He was about to leave when someone banged on the front door. His eyes shot to Gemma's, "Are you expecting anyone?"

"No," Gemma said wide-eyed as she followed Dean to the front door.

Dean ensured Gemma was safely behind him before opening it to find the police captain standing at the door and a sea of red and blue flashing lights in the driveway.

Chapter Seven

THE UNEXPECTED GUEST

"**G**ood evening, Doctor Walker and Mr. Singer," the police captain greeted them. "I'm sorry to disturb you so late." He eyed the two of them strangely. "But we got a call that someone was trying to break into the Singer's house."

"My grandparent's house?" Dean looked startled.

"Yes," the police captain said, craning his neck to see inside the manor house. "Are they here?"

"As you probably know," Dean said, stepping in his way so he couldn't enter the house. "My grandparents live around the side in Blueberry Cottage."

"Yes, of course," the police captain said. He turned towards the officer standing next to him and told him to check on the Singers. "Would you mind if we come inside and take a look around to be on the safe side?"

"Actually, I do," Gemma said. "I've been home the whole night and didn't hear anything."

Before Gemma could say any more, Dora and Paul came running up the front stairs, "Oh, thank goodness you're both alright." She embraced both Dean and Gemma at the same time.

"Pappy, Yaya, what is going on?" Dean asked them.

"I heard Rhino barking and barking," Paul told them. "I went to see what he was barking at, and a figure was trying to get into our kitchen window."

"So, your grandfather took the broom," Dora continued the story. "And the crazy old man went rushing after whoever it was."

"Oh, no," Gemma said. "Are you both alright?"

"We are fine," Dora assured her. "I was worried that whoever lurked about would try and get in here." She looked at Dean curiously, "Why are you here so late?"

"Gemma and I were discussing Patricia's will and some ideas for renovations to the manor," Dean lied.

"Ah," Dora's knowing eyes flashed approvingly. "Well, as Sophie is not home. I think you should stay here tonight just in case."

"Yaya," Dean said, "I'm sure Gemma is going to be fine."

"Uh, excuse me," the police captain said. "My men have checked the grounds, and whoever it was is long gone." He tried to see inside the manor once again. "If you are sure, you don't want us to have a quick search of the manor?"

"I think you should," Dora said before Gemma or Dean could decline the offer for a second time.

"If you don't mind the dog?" The police captain pointed to the officer standing with a German shepherd.

"Rhino is at my house," Dora told Gemma.

"Fine," Gemma said reluctantly since Dora had taken away her excuse of Rhino, and she didn't want to offend Dora, who was only looking out for her.

The police finally left twenty minutes later, and Dora, who insisted Dean stay the night, made up the room next to Gemma's. It had been a long crazy day full of adventure, experiences, memories, and shocking, life-changing revelations. But Gemma didn't feel alone for the first time in her life. Dean had been by her side through it all. He knew more about her after these three days than even her best friend of twenty-seven years, Terri did. Who would've thought the man that had spilled his coffee on her and had been so rude to her would've turned out to be the one person Gemma felt so free and comfortable with. She'd even broken into a house with him and enjoyed talking to him. Gemma had even found herself joking with and teasing him. She gave a small laugh. Terri would be really shocked.

Gemma's eyes flew open again as she realized she hadn't phoned Terri in two days. Nor had Gemma looked at her messages or checked her phone. She'd been so absorbed in everything going on in Honey Bay and with Dean that the time had flown by.

Gemma made a mental note to contact Terri in the morning. She had a lot to tell her, but Gemma wasn't quite ready to tell her just yet. She still couldn't quite get her head around that this was where her father had grown up. This was where she was born. She and her twin sister, Gabby, who, for some reason, Gemma called Dee. Dee, who had been her imaginary friend and who had saved her life. Then there was the mystery behind why her father had taken her away from her life here and left her sister behind. Gemma had a lot to sort through, and until she'd figured it out and made sense of it all, she wasn't ready to tell Terri.

Gemma rolled over and then grimaced, wishing she hadn't. Bruised ribs were not a good thing to have when trying to sleep. She pushed herself up carefully, propped up some pillows behind her, and found a comfortable position. Gemma closed her eyes again and sifted through the day's events. Trying to figure out how Gemma Walker from Los Angeles is supposed to reconcile with Gemmima Marshall from Honey Bay. Does she let go of Gemmima and continue as Gemma? How would she even begin to figure out who Gemmima Marshall is when Gemma left her behind twenty-eight years ago. Not only left her behind but forgotten her and everything from that time. Who is Gemma supposed to be now? Where does she go from here? Los Angeles felt like another lifetime ago, and Honey Bay was a minefield of questions, mysteries, and adventures.

When Gemma had come here three days ago, she had a clear goal. Find out how her father ended up with the Honey Bay estate. Now she had so many more questions. If Gemma's ribs weren't so sore, she'd turn over and punch the pillow. She couldn't even have a decent toss and turn right now. Gemma needed to try and get some sleep because there was no sense in trying to figure things out now at night when there was nothing she could do about them but fret. Tomorrow was another day on this crazy, beautiful island with Dean. His name conjured up his handsome smiling face and eyes, a multi-shade of blue from dark blue blazing anger, light compassionate blue, sparkling mischief sea blue, and deep caring blue. Gemma sighed as flashes of her time with Dean highlighted their crazy day and adventure-filled evening together. How their eyes locked and drew each other. The touch of his hand and then, of course, the gallant sweeping her off her feet and running up the sweeping staircase.

Gemma drifted off to sleep with Dean's handsome face in her mind. As her body relaxed, ready to shut down systems for the night and let her sleep ship take over, a sound caught Gemma's attention. Her body begged her to ignore it as it floated into her world of dreams, but her mind wouldn't let it go.

Gemma dragged her eyes open just in time to see a dark figure dash out of her room. Her breath caught in her throat, and she lay frozen in her bed, not knowing what to do. Something beside her moved, and she turned to see Rhino snoring next to her. Gemma shook her head in disbelief at the dog, who had once again snuck onto her bed. She pushed herself up and threw her legs over the edge of the bed, where she sat for a few seconds listening. There was nothing.

Could I have imagined it? Gemma's brow creased, and she decided she'd better check it out. She put her slippers on, pulled on her gown, and quietly headed towards her bedroom door. Gemma stood listening at the door for a few minutes before pulling it open. She stared into the dark for a moment before going back into her room to fetch her phone. Gemma put the light on, and something on the coffee table caught her eye. She went to pick it up and froze. It was the gold coin she'd given Gabby for her fifth birthday.

Gemma stood dead still, holding the coin up in the light. Something tingled up her spine when she realized who the hooded figure lurking around the grounds was. But she wasn't only lurking around the grounds but inside the house as well. Gemma's brow furrowed as she wondered why Gabby would leave the coin on the table. She drew in a breath as another question popped into her head — Had Gabby known Gemma was alive all this time? Or did she think Gemma was dead before she got here? Her eyes widened. Did her grandparents know she had been alive all this time? Gemma shook her head as she tried to shake the questions away. She was going to drive herself mad if she wasn't careful.

There were at least three people who could answer her questions. Two of them lived on the property, and the third was lurking around the house somewhere. Gemma shivered, thinking about someone lurking around the manor. What if it wasn't Gabby? The house was big. Too big.

For the first time since she got here, Gemma felt vulnerable. She palmed the coin and turned to look at her door, wondering if she should brave it and chase after the figure that had entered her room. If it was indeed Gabby... What if she wasn't looking for a sisterly reunion, and this coin was a warning? Gemma stood staring at the door. Maybe in the early morning hours, when everyone was asleep, it wasn't a good idea to find out if her sister had returned with friendly or hostile intentions.

Gemma decided she would rather wait for daylight. Clutching her phone and the coin, she went back to bed. She sat down and turned to get under the covers when a ball of fur hissed, growled, and slashed at her when she sat on it. Gemma jumped up and spun around, shining her light on her bed to see Victor with his hair standing on end, glaring at her. Gemma stood looking at the big cat in disbelief. The animal must enjoy tormenting her, Gemma thought.

"Shoo, Victor," Gemma waved her hand at him, but he didn't budge. Instead, he lay down on her pillow with his tail flicking warningly. "Get out of my bed." She stepped closer, grabbed a pillow, and waved at him. He gave her a warning growl. "Bad cat!" She hissed. "Shoo, get off my bed."

Her eyes narrowed on the cat. That was it! This animal had gone too far. Gemma reached down to pick him up, but he snarled and snapped at her. Gemma jumped back. She carefully pulled the comforter off the bed and took the pillow she'd managed to claim.

"You can sleep there tonight," Gemma told Victor. "But don't think I'm conceding because I'm scared of you or because I'm not a cat person. Which, by the way, is my right to be. Just like it's yours to be a grumpy cat." She turned to walk away and then turned back. "But this is not over." With that, she walked to the sitting area of her room. Gemma plopped the pillow on the sofa, wrapped herself in the comforter, and made herself as comfortable as possible.

"Gemma!" Dean's voice broke through the sleep fog. "Hey there, sleepy."

Gemma slowly opened her eyes and smiled, seeing Dean leaning over her. "Hi," Gemma greeted him. "What time is it?"

"It's still early," Dean whispered. "I just came to check on you because I heard a door close downstairs."

"A door?" Gemma sat up and grimaced. "Did you

come into my room earlier?"

"No, why?" Dean frowned.

"Oh, I thought I saw someone in my room earlier," Gemma saw the startled look in his eyes.

"Why didn't you come and get me?" Dean looked at her worriedly.

"I thought I may have dreamt it," Gemma looked at the hand she was sure she had held the coin in, but it was empty. Maybe it had been a dream.

"I tell you what, I'm going to get the spare mattress in the closet next door and sleep on the floor in your room tonight." Dean told her.

"You don't have to do that," Gemma told him, feeling silly for bringing up what she was now convinced was a dream.

"I'll feel better," Dean said. Then frowned. "Why on earth are you sleeping on the sofa?"

"Let's just say the bed was occupied." Gemma didn't want to admit to being kicked out of her bed by a cat. "They looked so comfortable I didn't have the heart to disturb them."

Dean shook his head and smiled, "You know you will have to show that cat who the boss is, or he's going to keep tormenting you."

"I did," Gemma lied. "I gave him a stern talking to." She stifled a yawn. "I have him under control and right where I want him."

"Really?' Dean said skeptically. "Because from where I'm standing, Victor and Rhino have your comfortable bed while you're on the small sofa. I'm guessing they have you in hand." He gave a small laugh and bent down to help her up. "Come on, I'll help you with your Victor problem."

She was starting to feel stiff from the day before, and her neck ached as she unraveled herself for the sofa.

"Just so you know," Gemma warned him. "I'm not practicing medicine at the moment, so if Victor decides you're the problem, I won't be able to patch you up."

Dean walked over to Gemma's bed, bent down, and picked up a docile Victor, who instantly started purring.

"Show off!" Gemma pulled a face at Dean, then glared at Victor, who she swore gave her a Cheshire cat grin. "Don't act all docile and sweet just because he's here." She said to the cat keeping her distance, though. She had enough scratches from him.

"Let's go, Mr. Meanie," Dean said to Victor. "You have to stop harassing Gemma." He looked at Rhino, who tried to hide beneath the covers, knowing he was next to be thrown off the bed.

"He can stay," Gemma said, stifling a yawn. "I find him quite comforting in this big old house."

"I'll take the menace and be back in a few minutes to camp out on your floor." Dean said and left her room.

Gemma slid back into her comfortable bed. She was so tired she hardly heard Dean walk quietly into the room.

"It's only me," Dean said in a low voice.

Gemma heard shuffling in the distance and then it went quiet.

"Night, Gemma." Were the last words she heard before drifting into a deep dreamless sleep feeling safe knowing Dean was close.

Gemma heard the buzzing from her alarm near her head. She reached out to her bedside table to pick up her phone, but it slipped from her fingers and fell on the floor. Gemma wasn't ready to wake up, so she left it there. She started drifting back to sleep when something tickled her cheek, and she slapped it away. Her eyes flew open when she felt something thick and creamy squash on her face. The smell of lilies and jasmine tickled her nostrils, and the sound of giggling drifted over her. Gemma knew that scent. Her eyes narrowed, and she lifted her hands into view. They were covered in Lady Shave.

Gemma sat up, wincing from her aching muscles, her eyes narrowed in on the petite blond woman, with a smug smile on her face and a giggling Sophie.

"Terri?" Gemma said to the woman, not sure if she was still dreaming or not. "What are you doing here?"

"Waiting for you to finally wake up." Terri told her.

"I see you've made a new friend," Gemma smiled at Sophie. "Hi, Sophie."

"Hi." Sophie waved and grinned.

"I needed a new one because it seems I've lost my old one." Terri raised her eyebrows. "She disappeared into the Bahamas. After not hearing from her for a few days, I thought she'd either been kidnapped, or there was no cellphone reception on the island. Turns out she was just being a bad friend and worrying her other friend half to death!"

"I'm sorry," Gemma said, feeling awful. "If it's any consolation, I was going to call you first thing this morning."

"Really?" Terri said, eyeing her skeptically. "Because it's almost ten-o-clock..." She picked up her phone and looked at it, showing Sophie. "Do you see any phone calls from Gemma, Soph?"

"No," Sophie said, shaking her head. "Shame on you, Doctor Walker."

"Do you know how many unanswered and unread calls and messages I have sent you?" Terri once again showed her phone to Sophie.

"Okay!" Gemma held up her slimy hands that she really needed to wash. "I get it, and I am really sorry. It's been hectic, and there has just been so much to take in." She looked at her hands and sighed. So much for not being ready to talk to Terri. "The shaving cream gag, Terri?" She glared at Terri and Sophie grinning.

"You're lucky it wasn't the honey gag," Terri pointed out.

"Can't you be like a normal person and just yell?" Gemma looked at her shaving cream covered hands.

"It's a lot more satisfying watching you smear shaving cream all over your face," Terri told her. "Besides you know I don't like to yell. I'm a psychiatrist. I encourage my patients to work through their issues in a healthier way."

"And playing pranks on sleeping people is healthy?" Gemma frowned.

"It's better than yelling." Terri pointed out. "Now get changed, and you can tell us all about your Honey Bay adventure over breakfast," Terri said, looking at Sophie. "Do you know any place that makes a great breakfast?"

"I do," Sophie told her. "Downstairs, my Yaya makes the best breakfast on the island."

Sophie jumped up and took Terri's hand, pulling her off the sofa.

"Oh, really?" Terri was being dragged out the door by Sophie. She turned and looked at Gemma. "Don't take too long. Sophie has promised to be our tour guide today."

"Sophie?" Gemma frowned, standing up and walking to the sitting area as it dawned on her she'd been so shocked to see Terri that she hadn't asked how she'd ended up with Sophie. "Where is her father?"

"Oh, the handsome lawyer?" Terri raised an

eyebrow. "He asked me to give you this." She pulled a folded note from her pocket, holding it out to Gemma. "I like him, by the way." She gave Gemma a knowing smile.

"Why didn't he send me a text?" Gemma took the note from her and glared at Terri,

"Because I told him you don't read those!" Terri had to rub it in a little more that Gemma had ignored her messages.

"Or you knew you couldn't unlock my phone and wanted to read what he was writing?" Gemma guessed.

Terri shrugged, "Sophie and I just wanted to make sure he was being nice." She batted her eyes innocently.

"Come on, Doctor Green, I'm starving," Sophie tugged on her hand.

"Oh, and we have Sophie for the day," Terri said, ducking out the door with her partner in crime before Gemma could ask any more questions.

Gemma stood staring at the door and wondering if she was still dreaming or not. She shook her head, closed her bedroom door, and was about to read Dean's note when her phone's message notification went off. Gemma walked around the bed to where it had landed on the floor and picked it up, freezing when she saw a message from an unknown number and a picture of the gold coin lying on the table in her room.

EPILOGUE

Good morning Gemma,

I hope you managed to get a good couple of hours of sleep. I'm sorry, but I will have to move our plans to tomorrow. I've had to go to Nassau to help Garrett and I won't be back until then.

If you're reading this, you know that your friend, Terri, from Los Angeles, arrived early this morning. I'm sorry to do this to you, and I hope you don't mind, but I need someone to look after Sophie until I'm back, and Terri volunteered.

My grandparents are going to stay with my aunt to help with the festival arrangements and Sophie gets so bored.

Thank you, Gemma.

Dean.

P.S. I'm looking forward to our date tomorrow.

Gemma's hands shook as she stared at Dean's note. It should've triggered a few reactions from her, with the last sentence making her warm fuzzy and smile. But her system was being overrun by a much more powerful emotion at the moment — fear! In one hand, she held a note from Dean, and in the other, her phone, which had beeped with two more messages right after the picture of the coin had appeared. The second one was a picture of Honey Bay café, and the third simply said — *9 pm. Alone!*

When she'd found the coin in the early hours of the morning, Gemma had wondered why Gabby had left it there and if it may have been some sort of warning or threat. After receiving the messages, Gemma couldn't help but feel it was a bit of both. She wasn't quite sure what to do and, to her surprise, Gemma wished Dean was here. Another message beeped, and she nearly didn't look at it, but it was from Terri, telling her to hurry up or they'd eat all the food.

Gemma knew she should move and needed to shower and change, but she couldn't even breathe properly, let alone move. Gemma was about to force herself to stand up and nearly dropped her phone when it rang. She fumbled to catch it with her shaky hands but did so before it hit the floor. Gemma grabbed her throbbing ribs and turned the phone to see it was Dean calling her.

She swallowed, cleared her throat, and answered the phone, trying to sound as normal as possible, "Hello?" Gemma said a little too brightly.

"Hi," Dean's voice flowed through the phone, making her feel a little more secure. "Sophie messaged me to let me know you were awake. I hope she didn't wake you?"

"No," Gemma lied. "Everything's fine." *Everything's fine?* Gemma pulled a face, not believing what she'd just said.

"Okay..." Dean said, and she could hear he knew something was up because Gemma didn't know how to put on a poker voice.

Was that a thing? A poker voice? Gemma thought nervously, then gave herself a mental shake. *Get a hold of yourself, Gemma.* She pinched the bridge of her nose, stood up from the bed, walked toward the bathroom, and stopped by the seating area. *Say something!*

"Did you get a good few hours of sleep?" Gemma rolled her eyes. Not *that! Why did you say that?* "I mean..." She swallowed. Gemma never stammered, and although she wasn't good at small talk, she wasn't usually a blithering idiot like she was right now.

"I did, thank you," Dean told her. "Gemma, is everything alright? You sound flustered or upset." He paused for a few seconds. "If you don't feel comfortable looking after Sophie..." He trailed off. "I can see if her sitter is available. With the fruit festival starting on Monday, my grandparents stay with Leigh in town to help with the organization. It is so busy, and Sophie gets so bored."

"Dean, it's okay!" Gemma finally managed to find a bit of rational thought to join some sensible words together. "Of course, I'll look after Sophie."

"Thank you." Dean could hear him breathe a sigh of relief. "She was very excited when your friend Terri offered your services."

"Thank you for seeing to Terri. I shouldn't have slept so long," Gemma said. "I had no idea Terri was planning a visit."

"She is quite a character and very protective over you, your friend, Terri," Dean told her.

"Oh no, what did she do?" Gemma looked up at the ceiling resignedly.

"Let's just say all the room we were in needed was a chair and a bright light shining in my eyes." Dean laughed.

"She interrogated you!" Gemma sighed. "I'm sorry."

"No, it was perfectly alright. I'm used to dealing with shrinks," Dean told her. "Besides, it gave me more confidence to leave my daughter with a total stranger before you woke up. Anyone as fiercely protective as Terri took her responsibilities seriously, and then Sophie took an instant liking to Terri."

"I think that's because they are so much alike," Gemma said through gritted teeth, feeling the crusty feeling of drying shaving cream on her hands. They both loved playing pranks on people.

They spoke for a few more minutes before Dean had to go, and Gemma was left feeling so alone after the call ended. She was about to go to the shower when she saw the gold coin peeking out between the sofa cushion where she'd fallen asleep with it in her hand. Gemma reached down, picked it up, and shuddered. She needed to put the messages from her mind and school herself to act as if her life wasn't a confusing mess at the moment.

The day flew by, and Sophie was such an easy child. She took them on a tour she called Sophie's Secret Island spots. They saw a new orchard on Fruit Island, where all the trees were mini trees that grew small fruit. They saw the small Honey Bay Aquarium, the seabird rescue center, Tony's touch farm, and ended the day taking a two-hour Island Horse Buggy tour. It was nearly six p.m. when they returned to the manor loaded with pizza for dinner, souvenirs from the day, and other items that Terri had bought for Sophie and herself.

They were no sooner through the door when Gemma got another message on her phone, and she nearly dropped the pizza when she saw it was from an unknown number. This time it showed a picture of Terri, Sophie, and her on the horse buggy tour. An icy shiver shot up her spine and she froze on the spot. Gemma had to quickly compose herself as Sophie came to fetch the pizza. Gemma knew without a doubt that it was not a warning but a threat.

By eight, they were all piled into Gemma's huge bed to watch a movie and were soon joined by Rhino and Victor, who took an instant liking to Terri. He hopped up onto her, flicking his tail. He walked over her to take a position between Terri and Sophie, where he lay all purringly sweet. Halfway through the movie, Terri, exhausted from traveling, fell asleep with Sophie in her arms and Victor, the menace, curled up between them. Gemma let them sleep. It was nice to have company after what had happened the previous night and that morning with the messages. Gemma's heart jolted with fear when she thought of the messages. She looked at the time on her phone, and it was a quarter-to-nine.

Panic and fear washed over her as she bit nervously on her thumbnail. She wondered what would happen if she didn't go meet Gabby? Surely, she wouldn't do anything silly like try to harm her or... Gemma looked over at Sophie and Terri, sleeping peacefully. More fear rushed through Gemma because she didn't know what Gabby was capable of. She remembered Dean warning her that Gabby would do whatever it took to get what she wanted. Gemma swallowed and squeezed her eyes shut. She knew she couldn't take a chance with Sophie and Terri's safety.

Gemma got up and quietly went to put on some jeans, a sweater, and sneakers. Rhino lifted his head and whined softly.

"Stay, Rhino!" Gemma commanded, and to her surprise, he actually listened. *Huh!* Gemma thought. *Dean was right. I need to be more commanding.* Like she was when she was Doctor Gemma Walker. Although she wasn't really sure who that was anymore. Gemma pushed thoughts of her identity crisis from her mind. Slipped the coin Gabby had left in her room into the pocket with her phone and quietly snuck out of her room, stopping in the kitchen to find a flashlight. Gemma found one in the broom closet before she slipped out the back door and headed into the night towards Honey Bay Café.

Gemma moved quickly towards the empty café where she had no idea what she'd be walking into. She wanted nothing more than to turn around and run like the wind back to the manor. Gemma felt like she was physically standing at the crossroads of her life as it was at the moment. Going back to the house felt symbolic of how Gemma had lived her life up until then. Sheltered in a cocoon protecting her from the truth of her past and instead of emerging from it she stayed in there hiding away from who she was supposed to be. Since she'd set foot on Honey Bay Gemma felt she had started to break free of the protection of her memory loss cocoon but was afraid to let go of it altogether. Going to the cafe would force her to confront her past so she could finally move forward and find out who she was meant to be.

As Gemma neared the café, she stopped, staring at its dark shape illuminated by the full moon hanging low over the dark ocean that felt like it was watching her as she walked. She shuddered and stood holding her breath while fear pounded from her heart like jungle drum signals warning her senses to turn and flee. She swallowed, standing on the precipice of pushing forward toward the haunting shadows of Honey Bay Café or running back to the safety of the manor.

The picture of the horse buggy trip popped into her head, reminding her that Gabby was not just lurking in the shadows of the manor but everywhere, waiting and watching. She had no choice. Gemma had to find out what Gabby wanted, and if her threatening messages were anything to go by, it was nothing good. Gemma squared her shoulders, took a deep breath, and walked towards the café. She got to the base of the stairs and could see a dull light glowing in the window, slightly to the right of the stairs. Gemma's hand shook as it touched wood, clammy from the sea air. She was just about to take the first step when her heart nearly exploded in fear when a gloved hand trapped her mouth, and she was pulled against the side of the café.

"Don't scream," an unfamiliar female voice whispered into her ear. "I'm going to take my hand away from your mouth, but you must keep very quiet."

Gemma had to move with the woman as she slowly backed her away from the Café and into the bushes behind it. "I need you to nod if you understand that you can't scream and need to keep still."

Gemma felt like she would pass out from holding her breath and the terror coursing through her. She honestly didn't know if she could scream and was surprised her legs hadn't collapsed as she'd moved away from the café with the woman. So, she did the only thing she could and nodded. The hand fell away from her mouth. Gemma spun around so fast that she nearly fell over the gloved hand shot to steady her.

"What part of you needed to be still and quiet wasn't clear?" The woman had a familiar black hoodie on, and Gemma's eyes widened when she lifted her head.

"You!" Gemma hissed.

"Not the family reunion I was hoping for," Gabby Marshall whispered. "But I guess it breaks the ice."

"Are you joking right now?" Gemma looked at her in disbelief. "You nearly scared me half to death, sneaking into my room and then sending me threatening messages demanding I meet here in the dead of night."

Gemma was flabbergasted at how cool Gabby was right now. They had just come face to face for the first time in twenty-nine-years and Gemma couldn't believe how flippant Gabby was. And what did she mean by a family reunion after she'd threatened

Gemma and bullied her into meeting her at the cafe in the dark?

Hot anger surged through Gemma as her eyes ran the length of the woman that was her mirror image and stopped when she saw what Gabby was wearing.

"Are those my favorite jeans?" Gemma looked accusingly at her and ran her flashlight over the black hoodie. "And that's my missing sweater!"

"Sorry, I had to borrow some clothes," Gabby said calmly, her brow creasing before her hand shot out. She snatched Gemma's flashlight, switched it off, then shoved it into her backpack. "I didn't have time to pack."

"Did you steal that backpack too?" Gemma asked. "I thought you were a cop, not a petty thief!"

"Borrowed!" Gabby corrected. "I borrowed the backpack from Dora and Paul. They won't mind."

"It was you breaking into their house last night," Gemma said incredulously.

"No, I didn't break into their house. I found an alternative way in when the doors were locked," Gabby corrected Gemma once again. Her brows furrowed, and she looked at Gemma with serious, narrowed eyes. "What did you mean?"

"Excuse me?" Gemma looked at her in confusion.

"You said I snuck into your room and sent you messages?" Gabby reminded her.

"Last night or rather early hours this morning, you snuck in and left this coin for me," Gemma fumbled in her pocket and pulled out the coin, shoving it at Gabby. "Then this morning, you sent me these?" She clicked her phone on and showed Gabby the messages. "Do you suffer from short-term memory loss or something?"

Gemma watched Gabby look at the three messages, her face void of expression, before she calmly handed Gemma her phone. Gabby lifted the coin, examining it in the moonlight. She looked at Gemma, and her expression stabbed even more fear into Gemma's heart. Then Gabby's following words paralyzed her with fear.

"Gemma, I didn't send you those messages," Gabby's voice was controlled. "And this is not my coin." She held it out in the palm of her hand. "It was yours."

THE SERIES CONTINUES

ARE YOU READY TO READ Honey Bay Cafe: Morning Lights book 4 of the Second Chance Mystery Series?

To read the next book in this series, go to www.amazon.com/B0BH75Q5Z3

HONEY BAY CAFE SPECIAL OF THE DAY

Aunt Autumn's Peach Cobbler

Preparation Time 1 hr.
  Serves 8 servings

TIPS

Canned peaches can be used with the recipe.

If canned peaches are used in the recipe, start the pie preparation at step no. 4

Dip the peaches into boiling water for a few seconds and then cold water to get the skin to peel off.

The dish is best served warm, straight from the oven with a scoop of ice cream, vanilla custard, or fresh cream.

INGREDIENTS

- 6 medium Peaches
- 1 cup Flour
- 1 tsp Baking powder
- 1 ½ cups Brown sugar
- ½ tsp ground Cinnamon
- ½ tsp Sea salt
- ½ cup Butter – unsalted
- 2 tbsp Peach juice
- ¾ medium fat milk

PREPARATION

1. Preheat oven to 350° F
2. Peel and core the peaches.
3. Slice the peaches into half-moon slices.
4. Over moderate heat, heat the sliced peaches in a heavy base medium saucepan with ½ cup of sugar and ¼ tsp sea salt.
5. Stir the peaches, sugar, and sea salt together and add the peach juice.
6. Cook the mixture until the sugar melts. Once cooked, remove the saucepan from the heat.
7. Melt the butter in the microwave.
8. Combine the remaining sugar and salt with the flour and baking powder in a mixing bowl.

9. Slowly fold the milk into the mixture until all the mixture is moist.
10. Using a 9 x 13-inch baking tray, pour the melted butter over the bottom of the dish, covering it evenly.
11. Pour the batter mixture evenly over the bottom of the buttered pan.
12. Place the peaches into the batter and drizzle the sauce over the top.
13. Sprinkle the ground cinnamon over the top of the peaches and sauce.
14. Place the pie in the oven and bake for 40 minutes or until golden brown.
15. Serve with your choice of ice cream, fresh cream, or vanilla custard.

Enjoy!

ALSO BY AMY RAFFERTY

Want to read more from *Amy Rafferty?*

To dive into your next read, go to https://www.amyraffertyauthor.com/

STAY UPDATED WITH ME

Thank you so much for purchasing or downloading my book! I am grateful to all my amazing readers.

To stay updated on all my latest books, newsletters, freebies and beautiful photos from the fabulous locations I write about, why not join my VIP group?

I will send you regular pictures of La Jolla Cove, San Diego and the Florida Gulf Beaches where I try to spend as much time as I can. I live in San Diego, my own 'Garden Of Eden' and I am in love with the sea and the beaches in the area. They inspire me to write lots of beachy mystery romance fiction to share with my awesome readers like you. To join me go to https://landing.mailerlite.com/webforms/landing/y6w2d2

You will be asked for your email. You also get a FREE BOOK whenever you sign-up!

FREE BOOK

To get your FREE copy of Cody Bay Inn Prequel - Nantucket Calling go to www.amazon.com/B0992NFTY1

ABOUT THE AUTHOR

Amazon #1 Best-Seller, Amy Rafferty is a contemporary romance author of feel-good beach romance reads with heartwarming stories embracing humor and love.

Born in New York, previously a Lawyer, she now lives in San Diego with her beautiful children and cats!

Aside from writing, publishing and running her home, she spends as much time as she can visiting the beautiful San Diego and Florida beaches where she has family and friends. She calls San Diego her 'Garden of Eden', inspiring her to write clean and wholesome romance novels incorporating mystery, suspense and adventures for her characters as they find a way to open their hearts and let true love in.

facebook.com/amyraffertyauthor
instagram.com/amyraffertyauthor

www.ingramcontent.com/pod-product-compliance
Lightning Source LLC
LaVergne TN
LVHW021224080526
838199LV00089B/5824